THE BILLIONAIRE'S KISS

THE SHERBROOKES OF NEWPORT

CHRISTINA TETREAULT

ISBN: 978-1-7352976-1-3

Digital ISBN: 978-1-7352976-2-0

CHAPTER 1

MOST DAYS, her condo's windows provided Juliette Belmont with an excellent view of Central Park and the city as a whole. Today gray skies and a torrential downpour that mirrored her mood obscured it. Closing her eyes, she pressed a palm against the cold glass while her mom continued to berate her over the phone. Well, perhaps berate was too harsh a word, but at the moment, Marilyn Belmont was sharing her true feelings and holding nothing back.

I get it, Mom. Can we move on now? Juliette resisted the urge to tell her mom to shut up. She might be an adult, but there were still some things you didn't say to your mother. Still, she wished her mom would put a sock in it. Especially since it wasn't as if Juliette didn't already know she'd royally screwed up. And if it was possible to travel back in time, she'd do so and tell Daniel Green to take a hike the night he approached her. But she couldn't change the past, and her mom's lecture only made her feel worse.

"I know you wanted to do some campaign work for your uncle, but under the circumstances, I think it'll be better to wait a little while." Mom had moved the conversation on to a slightly different topic, at least.

Uncle Warren, or President Warren Sherbrooke, as most of the world called him, certainly didn't need her help, but she'd been looking forward to assisting him. Unlike many of her family members, she hadn't helped with his campaign efforts the first time he ran for president. Now that he was running for a second term, she wanted to do her part.

"Your dad agrees with me," her mom continued.

Wow, big surprise. Her parents—whom she adored—rarely disagreed on anything.

Juliette rolled her eyes and looked at the ceiling. The way her parents were acting, one would think she'd committed armed robbery or something.

"This should all be old news in another month or two, and then you can help out."

Juliette hoped so. Although accustomed to having her face on the covers of magazines and all over the internet, she wasn't used to such negative publicity. And that was all she'd been getting since the first photos of her and Daniel and the story came out.

"I'll let Francine know I won't be attending the fundraiser this weekend," Juliette said, finally able to get a word into the conversation. Up until now, she'd managed only a handful.

"Great. And once this little situation passes, your uncle will be delighted to have your help. While I have you on the phone, have you thought any more about coming to work at the foundation?"

Ever since her older sister, Courtney, had taken a position at the Helping Hands Foundation, her mom had been after her to join them. While the foundation was a wonderful organization and she didn't mind helping with its various fundraisers, she wasn't sure she wanted to work there full-time.

If she was being truthful, she wasn't entirely sure what

she wanted to do anymore. She had no intention of admitting that to her mom. While Marilyn had never come right out and said it, Juliette knew her mom wished she'd pursued a career in something other than modeling—a career she'd loved until recently.

Nope, if it'd been up to her parents, she would have joined Sherbrooke Enterprises like her older brother and so many of her cousins after graduating from Columbia with a degree in marketing and a minor in dance—a degree she'd only pursed because her dad thought attending Columbia was a far better idea than Juilliard, her first choice of colleges.

Not that any of it mattered now, because she had a career most could only dream of, and if she woke up tomorrow and decided she needed a complete career change, she could have a position at Sherbrooke Enterprises with only a simple phone call. Honestly, though, any position that required she spend hours sitting behind a desk didn't appeal to her, and she didn't know how other people did it.

Since the weather made it impossible for her to enjoy the view, she turned away from the window. "A little, and I'm going to pass at least for now, Mom."

"Well, if you change your mind, my offer stands." A hint of disappointment laced her voice, but she didn't press the issue. "Can we expect to see you soon?"

Although she called New York City home, she spent a decent amount of time at her parents' house in Massachusetts. At the moment, she had no desire to be there. "I'll let you know."

Before her mom posed any additional questions, the doorbell rang, saving her. Few people visited her without calling first. "Mom, I need to go. Someone is at the door. I'll call you later this week."

After disconnecting the call, Juliette left her cell phone on an end table and crossed the living room.

Please don't be Scott. She adored her older brother, but this afternoon she wasn't up to facing him. He'd called her Wednesday after the first pictures of her and Daniel hit the internet. She'd let his call go to voice mail. The message he left merely said to call him, so she didn't know what his take was on her current scandal. But her brother was as straitlaced as they came. Never in his life had the media printed anything negative about the guy.

Holly Lambert, who lived on the floor below her, stood on the other side of the door. She'd met Holly while doing her first runway show in Milan. At the time, Holly had already been on her way to being a household name even though she had only started modeling the previous year. They'd been close friends ever since.

While Holly regularly visited and never called first, Juliette hadn't expected to find her ringing her doorbell today. The last time they spoke, Holly was vacationing in Anguilla.

"Hey, when did you get home?" She stepped back so Holly could enter.

"Yesterday. I thought about coming up to see you, but it was late." Holly didn't wait for Juliette to tell her to make herself comfortable before entering the kitchen and switching on the single-cup coffee machine. She treated Juliette's condo as her second home. Actually, she spent more time at Juliette's than she did her place.

"You saw the pictures?"

Holly nodded. "Did you really not know he was married?"

The comment caused her to grind her teeth together. She would have thought Holly knew her better than that. Sure, she dated a lot and rarely stayed in any one relationship for too long, but she never played the role of the other woman. There were plenty of single men in the world, so she saw no need to spend time with married ones.

Juliette shook her head. "It's not like I have a background check done on every man I go out with, and he never wore a ring." In the future, perhaps she should, though, and save herself from facing this issue again.

"But didn't you ever see any hints of a woman at his house? Clothes in the closet, makeup remover in the bathroom?" Holly removed a cup from the cabinet and pressed the brew button on the coffee machine. "She must have stuff there."

She hadn't been thinking about a coffee, but now that she smelled it, she wanted a cup. Juliette retrieved her favorite mug from the cabinet and placed it under the machine before selecting a dark roast coffee pod from the stand.

"I didn't exactly go snooping in his closets, Holly. And we spent a lot more time here than we did at his place."

"Next time you get involved with a man, maybe you should take a peek." Holly sipped her coffee and leaned back against the counter. "Considering all the time you spent together, I'm surprised Daniel's wife didn't learn about you two sooner."

"She's been in England for the past two months because her grandmother was ill—or at least that's the story the media is printing."

The media often altered the truth to suit its own narrative, but on this account, she saw no reason not to believe that Daniel's wife had only arrived in the United States recently. However, the woman must have suspected her husband was fooling around while alone in New York if she hired a private investigator to follow him.

Holly took another sip of her coffee before speaking again. They both tended to drink more coffee than was probably good for them. "Did she really find you together at his house?"

The media had left little out of the stories it had published so far. Juliette nodded and then gestured toward the living room with her coffee cup. Holly wouldn't let the matter go until she got the whole story, and Juliette would prefer to be sitting while she gave it. Holly took the hint and headed for the other room.

"We were in the middle of dinner when she came home. To say Daniel was shocked would be an understatement." Crossing her legs in front of her on the sofa, Juliette sipped her coffee as an image of Daniel's face when he first saw his wife came to mind. Under different circumstances, it would've been funny.

"He tried to play it off that we were business associates. As if anyone would believe that. Of course, Katherine knew the truth before Daniel opened his mouth. At some point in the past month or so, she'd hired a private investigator. She tossed at least a dozen photos of Daniel and me together at us. Some were taken inside the house, so I guess the person she hired somehow set up cameras in Daniel's place."

Holly grimaced. "Well, it could've been worse. She could've come home while you were both naked and in bed."

Yep, that would have been far worse. "After Katherine tossed my glass of chardonnay in my face, she told Daniel to expect to hear from her lawyer."

"I would've thrown it in Daniel's face instead. He's the one really to blame, not you. Anyway, what happened after that?"

"She left. I stuck around long enough to wash my face and get my coat and purse. Daniel kept going on about how screwed he was. I'm guessing they have a prenup, and it has a clause addressing infidelity. Prenups often do."

"Makes sense." Holly kicked off her shoes and tucked one leg under her. "According to the article in *Today Magazine,* Katherine's father is not only an English baron but a member of the House of Lords. Daniel's father is the current

Viscount of... honestly, I don't remember and worth millions. People with that kind of background wouldn't get married without a prenup."

Juliette didn't agree. While she knew prenups weren't uncommon among couples in her social circle, none of her cousins or siblings had ones prepared before getting married.

"Have you heard from him?"

She swallowed her mouthful of coffee and set her cup down. "Nope, and I don't want to."

"I never really liked him. He was always a little too..." Holly paused and tapped her fingers against the arm of the sofa. "Something. I don't know what."

She found it odd Holly never said anything. Holly wasn't known for keeping her opinion to herself. "At this point, I just want to forget about the whole thing. Which we both know is easier said than done, thanks to the media. When I tried to go out yesterday, three photographers were hanging around outside the building. I turned around and walked back inside."

"I saw one hanging around when I came back this morning. If he's still out there, I hope he forgot to bring an umbrella with him."

Juliette knew the lengths some paparazzi would go to get a picture, and they included standing in a downpour on a cold late-February afternoon.

"You, my friend, need a vacation. Someplace where the media or anyone else won't bother you."

She'd been contemplating a vacation for some time. She'd hoped a change of scenery would help her reassess her life. Even before her brother's wedding in November, she'd been unsatisfied with the status quo. When her sister had announced back in January that she was engaged, the feeling picked up speed, and now it plagued her every day.

"Sounds fabulous. Too bad I can't think of anywhere that fits that description."

Since all of her favorite vacation spots were also popular among Hollywood's elite, photographers were always lurking, ready to snap a photo when you least expected it. Not only that, she also didn't want to be around a lot of people, once again making all her usual destinations out of the question.

"If you know of any, feel free to share." Juliette took the last sip of her coffee and stood. "I'm making another cup and getting some lunch. Do you want anything?"

"I can make more coffee. And I'll have whatever you're eating."

Unlike her brother, who knew his way around the kitchen, Juliette didn't possess too many culinary skills. Still, even she could manage a garden salad, and she always had grilled chicken included in her weekly grocery deliveries.

Holly followed her toward the kitchen and made a beeline for the coffee machine. "I might know of someplace you could go where the media wouldn't bother you. Really, I don't think anyone would bother you. But it's nothing like the places you usually visit."

She'd consider almost anywhere if it meant no nosy photographer or reporters. "As long as it doesn't involve a tent out in the middle of a forest, I'm open to suggestions." She'd forgo access to a beach or five-star spas, but she drew the line at not having a comfortable bed and a roof over her head.

"Avon, New Hampshire," Holly answered, joining Juliette at the kitchen island and setting down both coffee cups. "There is a campground on the northernmost part of Avon Lake. It's owned by the Wright family. They close up most of the cottages in the fall, but a few they rent out year-round. There's a ski resort about twenty-five minutes away, and skiers will sometimes stay there instead of the resort because it's cheaper."

An image of a log cabin with no running water or electricity in the middle of a campground came to mind. "Yeah, I can live without room service, but I need running water and heat, Holly."

"It's not some rustic campground. All the cottages have everything a house would. Some even have two or three bedrooms. And they all have access to the lake, although it'll still be too cold at this time of year to swim in. It might even still have some ice on it. And even if we don't ask Mrs. Wright not to share that you're there, she won't email the *Star Insider* or announce your arrival on Twitter the minute you check in. She's not like that." Holly snagged a grape tomato from the plastic container and popped it in her mouth.

A cottage overlooking a lake somewhere up in northern New Hampshire sounded rather lovely. More than once, Holly had shared details about the small town she'd lived in until moving to New York, and it did sound charming.

"I can call Mrs. Wright and make reservations for you. She knows me. She and my mom are friends, and her youngest daughter and I were friends all through school. We still text each other every once in a while."

Juliette considered her friend's suggestion. If Holly believed she wouldn't be bothered, she trusted her assessment. And while the town might be small and in the middle of nowhere, it wasn't as if she planned to relocate there permanently. "Are the cottages close together?"

Holly had said not many people stayed there this time of year, but on the off chance others were there, she didn't want any neighbors staying mere feet away.

"Unless they've changed things since I was last there, it depends on the one you stay in." She grabbed a slice of cucumber off the cutting board. "If you're worried about neighbors, you could always stay in one cottage and rent out the ones on either side of you. That's what I'd do."

Juliette added an equal portion of cucumbers and tomatoes to each bowl before reaching for the bag of shredded carrots. "Exactly what I was thinking." Depending on how many cottages were available right now, maybe she'd just rent them all out for the next two or three months and guarantee she had the place all to herself.

"If you have the number, I'll call before we eat lunch." The sooner she made reservations, the sooner she'd get away from the city.

CHAPTER 2

Aaron logged out of his email and closed his laptop. Quasi-vacation or not, work emails never stopped. While some he could leave until he returned home, others required more immediate attention. With all those out of the way, he considered himself free for the rest of the day.

"Uncle Aaron, Dad says breakfast is ready," his eleven-year-old nephew, Mason, called from the other side of the door.

Since he was attending a conference in South Carolina anyway, he'd decided to fly down a few days before the conference started and visit his older sister and her family. While not exactly a vacation in some tropical location or Europe, the visit gave him a break from his normal routine and allowed him to spend time with people he saw far too little. And as much as he loved every minute here, sometime soon, he needed a true vacation. One that included either doing nothing on a warm beach while soaking up the sun or seeing all the historical sites in Europe he still hadn't checked off his very long list—a list he'd started to compile while in high school. So far, he'd only crossed off a handful of places in England.

After shoving his cell phone in his back pocket, Aaron opened the door, not at all surprised Mason was nowhere to be seen. If there was food in the kitchen, the kid would be there filling up his stomach. In that regard, his nephew reminded him of himself at that age.

The scent of bacon greeted him before he reached the kitchen. The popular breakfast meat might not be the healthiest thing in the world, but man, it tasted and smelled heavenly—at least to him. His younger sister would disagree.

As he expected, Mason sat at the kitchen table shoveling food into his mouth as fast as humanly possible while Aaron's older sister, Elise, sat across from him sipping coffee and reading a magazine. Elise looked like a younger version of their mom. In fact, if he looked at pictures of their mother at Elise's age, you'd think Elise had somehow traveled back in time and sat for the photos. That being said, Elise inherited none of their mom's skills in the kitchen. The woman ruined even oatmeal, and forget about something as simple as a grilled cheese sandwich. Thankfully, her husband possessed all the skills his wife didn't and prepared most of the family's meals. At the moment, he stood at the stove cooking pancakes.

Aaron snagged a slice of bacon off the plate on the table on his way to the coffeepot over by the stove.

"Is the next batch done?" Mason asked after he stuffed a forkful of pancakes in his mouth.

"Almost, but your uncle gets first dibs." Nick flipped a golden-brown pancake and glanced over at him. "Aaron, these have blueberries in them, but I can make some without if you want."

"As long as you're the one making them and not my sister, I'll eat whatever you put in front of me."

"Hey, your sister is getting better. She managed toast last week."

"I'll take your word for it." Aaron added a generous amount of cream and sugar to his coffee—no self-respecting New Englander drank it any other way—before sitting down at the table. "I can't believe you read that—"

He caught himself before he finished, although Aaron suspected his nephew heard a lot worse than the four-letter word he had in mind while on the school bus. At least he'd heard much worse when he rode the bus at Mason's age. Still, it never hurt to be more selective with one's language.

"—stupid magazine." He didn't understand why anyone cared what people with more money than brains did on a daily basis.

Nick set a plate full of pancakes on the table and grabbed a slice of bacon. "I ask her the same thing."

Elise closed the magazine and grabbed her son's hand before he stuck his fork in the newest stack of pancakes on the table. "If either of you bothered to read it, you'd know *Today Magazine* isn't a tabloid like *The Star Insider,* and it doesn't just publish celebrity pieces. Besides, it has great crossword puzzles every week."

Before his nephew made a second attempt for more food, Aaron took three pancakes and added them to the bacon on his plate. Then he pointed his fork toward the magazine. "Could've fooled me."

A photo of a gorgeous blonde he'd seen on countless covers while standing in the checkout line at the super-market occupied much of the magazine cover. Below the too-perfect face—no doubt the publication removed any imperfections prior to publication—was the headline "Caught In The Act." Then, in the bottom left corner, there was a smaller picture of a man and—he assumed—the same blonde woman kissing. At the same time, a picture of another woman and who he guessed was the same dark-haired dude as in the left-hand picture occupied the bottom right corner. And while there was also a photo in the top right of a Connecticut high school student who'd started a program that helped the less fortunate get prom dresses, the main headline, unfortunately, overshadowed it. Even without opening the magazine, he assumed he'd find more photos of the blonde with the dark-haired man and a story about how the guy had been caught cheating on the brunette with the blonde. After all, it seemed to be the norm among celebrities.

"The story about Juliette Belmont isn't the only one in there." Elise added another pancake to her plate and poured maple syrup over it.

"Let me guess, she's an actress and got caught with a married man?"

Elise shook her head, her expression asking what rock he'd been living under. "A model and President Sherbrooke's niece."

And those two facts make her so much more important than everyone else. If he'd been about twenty years younger, he would've rolled his eyes. Instead, he stuffed a forkful of food in his mouth.

"When are we leaving?" Mason asked.

He'd promised to take his nephew to the science museum today. Since Mason lived more than a thousand miles away, he didn't spend as much time as he'd like with him. A day at the museum would give him a chance to spoil his nephew while giving his older sister and her husband some time alone. It seemed like a win-win for everyone.

"Let your uncle at least eat his breakfast," Elise said. "And while he does, why don't you go upstairs and work on cleaning your room."

He'd seen his nephew's room. It'd take some effort and

maybe some heavy machinery before it even resembled moderately neat.

As expected, Mason frowned. "But, Mom—"

His sister's eyebrows inched up, and she blinked a few times. Aaron remembered their mom doing the same thing when she was about to deliver a statement they weren't going to like. "If you'd rather stay home today and work on your room, that's fine with me."

Mason gulped down the rest of his milk and pushed back his chair. "I'll go work on it now."

Aaron suppressed a grin. "Don't worry. I'll come and get you as soon as I'm done, buddy." Picking up his empty coffee cup, he stood. "You should get the kid a bulldozer to clean his room. Does it even have a floor?" He hadn't known where to step when he went in the other day. Clothes, books, and various pieces of sports equipment covered whatever parts of the floor that weren't occupied by furniture. "Do you want more coffee?"

With a nod, Elise handed him her cup. "Believe it or not, I helped him clean it a few weekends ago."

If Elise said she'd helped Mason, he'd take her word for it, because it looked like the room hadn't been touched in years.

"What do you two plan to do while we're gone?"

"A round of golf and then we have dinner reservations." Nick put another stack of pancakes on the table and took the seat across from his wife. "We haven't golfed together since the fall."

The cell phone next to his sister's plate chimed. As a certified midwife, the woman was never far from her phone.

Accepting her coffee, she picked up the device and glanced at the text message. "Mom said someone called yesterday and rented all five cottages for the next three months."

Although his mom closed up the majority of the cottages around the lake after the second weekend in October and didn't open them again until the first weekend in May, she always kept five open. Some years people rented them out every weekend during ski season, and other years the cottages remained empty for weeks on end. During the summer, it wasn't unusual for a group of relatives to rent out cottages so they could vacation together, but never this time of year. And as far as he could remember, no one had ever rented out a cottage for such a long period of time. But he knew his mom wouldn't complain, because the agreement would guarantee extra revenue.

"Mom must be happy. Did she say how many people she is expecting?"

Two of the larger cottages still open each accommodated up to six people, assuming two people slept in each bedroom and two people slept on the pull-out sofa. The other three cottages available in the winter each had one bedroom and a sleeper sofa.

"One," Elise answered.

"One person needs five houses? Who's staying there, the Queen of England?" Nick asked.

His brother-in-law made an excellent point. If an individual had rented out all the available cottages, they either didn't want any neighbors or they considered themselves superior to the rest of society.

"What do you think I'm asking her now?" Elise didn't look up as she typed out a new message. When she finished, she set the device down and reached for her fork. "But whoever it is, Mom expects them tomorrow."

ALTHOUGH SHE'D GROWN up in New England and still spent a fair amount of time there, Juliette could probably count on two hands the number of times she'd visited New Hampshire. And many of those times involved visits to see her cousin who'd moved to the state the previous year. During those visits to Pelham, she'd thought the town was rural. The more she drove through Avon, the more she realized how wrong she'd been about where her cousin lived. While Pelham had some small farms and a charming town green, it also had one fast-food restaurant, a chain coffee shop, and two traffic lights. So far, she'd seen no sign of any of those things here.

"You want to take the next left," Holly instructed her.

Since Holly hadn't seen her family in months, she'd offered to make the drive with her. She planned to stay with her parents for a little while and then catch a flight back to New York.

Juliette turned onto a road that actually had a sidewalk and a street sign. They'd crossed into town about ten minutes ago, and many of the streets she'd traveled so far were unmarked. Evidently, the town didn't want to make it easy for outsiders to find their way around.

Judging by the buildings lining both sides of the road, Main Street was the heart of Avon. On the right-hand side, a large municipal complex stood. The sign out front stated it housed the town hall, the police station, and the fire station. A store called Gorham's Shop and Save was across the street from the complex. It shared its parking lot with a small movie theater and a liquor store. Considering the old-school marquee listing the four movies currently being shown mounted over the entrance, she didn't expect to find any luxury loungers or IMAX screens inside. A mom-and-pop-style diner and coffee shop completed the businesses on the left side of the road. Not long after passing the municipal complex, she spotted a series of school buildings and the town's public library.

"Let me guess, this is considered downtown," she said as they passed the post office and a hair salon.

"There are a few other businesses scattered around town, but yeah, I guess you'd consider this the downtown area. It makes 5th Avenue look dull, doesn't it?" Holly asked, laughing. "It's not as bad as you think. We don't have many retail businesses here, but North Conway is only about forty minutes away. You can find just about anything you need there. And since it tends to be a popular tourist destination, they also have some nice little artist studios and boutiques. Ashford, the next town over, has some restaurants and shopping as well."

She'd have to keep a visit there in mind for another day because once she got out of the car today, she had no intention of getting back inside it.

"Unless you want to do a little exploring, you'll want to take a right at the stop sign."

She wouldn't mind getting a better look at the town she planned to call home for the next few months. However, they'd spent roughly seven hours in the car today, and she needed another bathroom break. "Maybe I'll do some tomorrow."

A few miles and a handful of turns later, she got her first glimpse of Avon Lake. "I expected the lake to be much smaller." Why, she didn't know, but she'd expected it to be about the same size as the one not far from her cousin's house. The body of water on her left was at least fifty times larger, if not more.

Holly reached for her purse, pulled out her cell phone, and typed a message. "This is the third-largest lake in the state. If you ask my brother, he can probably tell you exactly how many acres it covers and how deep it is. All I know is it is huge. Right now, we're on the southernmost portion of it," Holly explained as they drove.

Homes of various sizes and ages dotted the shore. Several had docks leading into the water, and when the temperatures warmed up, Juliette assumed boats would be parked alongside many of them. The houses continued for several miles before they stopped and were replaced with trees for a short time before ending at a public beach.

"The easternmost side is actually part of Ashford. There are several restaurants right on the water over there. In the summer, people will take their boats out for a few hours and then stop at one of them for lunch or dinner. And if we'd turned onto Timberlane Road instead of Harris, we eventually would have reached the kids' summer camp along the western section of the lake. I used to love going there."

Since the street signs remained sparse, she didn't know which roads Holly referred to—not that it really mattered. She didn't need a summer camp.

"Besides the campground, is there anything else where we're headed?"

"Nope. The Wrights own almost all the land and have for about a hundred years or so. Again, if you ask my brother, he'll know. He's a walking textbook of town facts."

The sound of a rooster crowing came from the device in Holly's hand. Why her friend used such an annoying sound to alert her to text messages was a mystery to Juliette.

"Mom's on her way. My sister is with her."

When Holly had informed her mom she was headed home and explained the reason why, Eleanor offered to go grocery shopping so Juliette wouldn't need to worry about it. Although fully capable of doing the task herself, she'd accepted the offer immediately, since it meant she could avoid any public places for at least a little while. The food and other items Eleanor picked up wouldn't last forever, but perhaps by the time she needed to replace them the media would've found a new juicy story to focus on.

"How long do you think you'll stay with your parents?"

Eleanor and Holly's twin brother, Marc, frequently visited New York, so she knew them both well. She'd only met Holly's dad and sister a handful of times. Regardless, she knew the Lamberts were a close-knit family much like hers. But no matter how much you adored your family, after a while you usually wanted to get away from them. At least that tended to be the case for her. Holly had a similar personality, so she didn't see it being any different for her.

"A few days. A month. I don't know. I might even go visit my cousin in Maine before I head back home."

"Is that the one who had a baby in September?" They hadn't passed a single house in about ten minutes, and Juliette kept a lookout for any signs they were almost at their destination.

"Yes. And right before Valentine's Day, she and her husband moved into the house they spent the last eight months building. The road you want is about another mile or so on the right."

Unfortunately, the information didn't help her much. She'd never been great at determining distance. When she received any kind of directions, she needed landmarks, not the number of miles she needed to travel before turning left or right. And forget about telling her to drive east or west. Unless the words were attached to specific streets in the city, they had no meaning to her.

Eventually, a road came into view on her right. A sign with the words Wright's—Private Way hung from a pole.

Holly gestured toward the road before slipping her cell phone back into her purse. "This is the road you want."

Calling this dirt path a road was a bit of stretch, but at least it was well maintained.

After rounding a curve in the road, a large shingle-sided home came into view. While her taste in homes tended to lean more toward either a contemporary design or something more like her parents' home, she couldn't deny that this style so often found along the ocean in places like Newport and Martha's Vineyard fit its surroundings. Actually, it reminded her of a smaller version of Walker's Point Estate in Kennebunkport, Maine.

She pulled in next to a Honda Accord already parked in an extended portion of the driveway marked Guest Parking.

"That's Mom's car. She must be inside talking to Mrs. Wright. They've been friends since elementary school."

Her dad's home office in Weston was larger than the one she followed Holly into. Then again, perhaps a large space wasn't required for running a campground. Despite the size, it was tastefully decorated.

Holly's mom and sister greeted them both with hugs the moment they entered. She'd learned early in their friendship that Holly's mom was a hugger. In fact, she'd hugged her the very first time they met. Evidently, Mrs. Wright was as well, because she came from behind her desk and embraced Holly.

"It's great to see you," Mrs. Wright said before turning her attention Juliette's way and extending her hand. "Welcome. I have a few things for you to sign, and then I can show you down to your cottage."

She expected a handful of papers to read through and sign; instead, the owner retrieved an iPad and stylus from her desk. While she glanced through agreements, Mrs. Lambert and Tara, Holly's sister, filled Holly in on something that had occurred in town the previous week. Considering the surprised look on Holly's face, she knew the parties involved.

Juliette waited until there was a slight break in their conversation before holding out the iPad. "All set."

Mrs. Wright returned the device to her desk and selected

five keys from the wall. "All five cottages are fairly close together. I thought we could drive down there, and you can pick the one you want?"

Judging by the way Holly described them, all the cottages were similar. "No, that's fine. Just pick one for me." It wasn't like she planned to spend the rest of her life living here.

The woman returned all but one key ring to its hook. "Cottage 10 is my favorite."

Juliette had checked out the campground's website after making the reservations. Although the pictures looked great, she'd still been a little apprehensive on the ride here today. She knew full well how much a photo could be manipulated. As she followed Holly's mom down to the cottage, she saw that in some ways the pictures on the website hadn't done the place justice. Although they varied in size and some were closer together than others, all the buildings looked like they'd been constructed in the past year, which thanks to Holly and the brief history on the website, she knew wasn't true.

Mrs. Lambert's car stopped in front of a cottage with the number 10 on the front door. Painted white with dark gray shutters and a matching door, it wasn't as large as some of the others they'd passed, but it had a front porch with a swing. It also had an unobstructed view of the lake, something not all the others had. Immediately, she pictured herself sitting out on the swing in the morning and drinking her coffee. As much as she loved all the things she could do in Manhattan, sipping coffee from her front porch while looking at the water wasn't one of them.

Before she opened the car door and joined the other women, she glanced at Holly. "Thank you. I think this is just what I need."

Juliette had seen her share of beautiful interiors, but she'd never seen anything quite as quaint as the inside of the cottage—and the word quaint was the only way to describe the place. The main entrance opened into the living room, which transitioned into a small kitchen. On her left, a staircase that hugged the wall led to the second floor, while on her right stood a woodstove.

"This cottage only has one bedroom upstairs. I don't know if you plan to have any guests while you're here, but that's a sleeper sofa." She pointed toward the blue-and-white gingham sofa. "But if you want something larger, cottages 6 and 4 have two bedrooms."

Nope, she didn't expect any overnight visitors. While the primary purpose of this getaway was to avoid media, it was also about her having some time alone to make some decisions. As much as she loved her family, she'd find that difficult to do if they came and spent the night. "This is perfect."

"Excellent. There's a binder in the kitchen with some information you might find useful, including the restaurants near us that deliver. If you want to use the woodstove, you can go to Valley Landscaping and get some wood, or you can call them; they'll deliver it to you. Both their address and phone number are in the binder as well."

She'd done a lot of things in her life, but starting a fire wasn't one of them. While she doubted it was difficult, she didn't see herself giving it a try anytime soon.

"If you need anything or have any issues, please just call."

CHAPTER 3

AFTER SLEEPING in his sister's spare bedroom for a few days and then in a hotel room for several more, Aaron was looking forward to a night in his own bed. While the hotel he'd stayed at had been great and offered guests some excellent amenities, including one of the nicest indoor pools he'd ever used, at the end of the day, he'd still returned to a hotel room. The same was true of his stay at his sister's house. Although Nick and Elise had insisted he treat the place as his own and even gave him a key, it wasn't the same as being in your own home.

Perhaps even more than his bed, he was looking forward to a meal that didn't come from a restaurant. The last home-cooked meal he'd eaten had been breakfast on Sunday before leaving his sister's house for the conference in Charleston. He enjoyed eating out as much as the next person, but it got old fast when you did it for every meal.

Rubbing the persistent ache over his left eye, he stopped at the four-way intersection. While he did a fair amount of air travel each year, he hated it. Between the long lines at security, cramped seats onboard the plane, and frequent delays thanks to the weather, it often gave him something bordering on a migraine and put him in a foul mood. Today's travel experience hadn't been any different. After making his way through security this morning, he'd sat around the airport for an additional two hours, thanks to a weather delay. Then he'd hung around the airport in Nashville for another hour and a half. He never understood who planned the flight routes. To him, it made very little sense to fly west and then north, but that particular flight had been one of the cheapest available. Even when his plane landed, his traveling wasn't done, thanks to the almost three-hour drive from Boston to Avon. Actually, the only time he missed living in the city was when he flew in and out of Logan Airport.

Thankfully, his day of travel was just about behind him, and he didn't need to head back to Boston for at least two weeks.

The guitar solo pumping through the car's speakers stopped, replaced by the ringtone he'd programmed for when his younger sister called. When he answered, though, it wasn't Candace that greeted him. Instead, it was his niece, Tiegan.

"Hi, Uncle Aaron. Mom wants to know if you'll be home for dinner."

For the past seven months, his sister and niece had been living with him. On the nights Candace didn't have class, she prepared dinner. Unlike their older sister, she cooked as well as, if not better, than their mom.

"Yep. Tell her I'm less than five minutes from home."

Growing up, he'd looked forward to calling somewhere other than Avon home—not that he didn't love the town, but he'd been eager to leave and experience somewhere different. As soon as he graduated college, he'd gotten his first apartment in Watertown. He'd lived there until he could afford a condo in Boston just minutes from his office. Three years ago, though, he'd bought his parents' house and moved back to town. He didn't regret his decision in the least. Well, except for days like today when he traveled. If he still lived in Boston, he would've been home hours ago and already relaxing in front of the television with a beer.

"Okay. I'll tell Mom. We made lasagna and meatballs." His niece loved to help in the kitchen, and it didn't matter who was doing the cooking or what they were making.

Even after three years of owning the home, sometimes when he drove up, he thought of it as his parents' house—the place where he and his sisters had grown up rather than a place that belonged to him. Especially when he'd been away for any length of time. His dad had never mentioned it, but Aaron wondered if he'd felt the same way after inheriting the house, the land, and everything on it.

No lights appeared in the windows of the apartment over the campground office. More than likely, it meant Mom was joining them for dinner—something she often did. He still had mixed feelings about her living there. The house was big enough for her to live with him. And when his dad died and Aaron purchased the home, he'd insisted she stay. But she'd been adamant about him having his own place and had the space over the campground office converted into a one-bedroom apartment.

It wasn't the only thing she'd been adamant about. When he'd first mentioned he planned to move back to Avon so he'd be close by in case she needed him, she'd insisted it wasn't necessary, that she didn't want him disrupting his life because of her. He'd ignored her because the idea of her being alone with so many strangers coming and going from the property bothered him. Once he'd convinced her nothing she said would change his mind, he'd started looking for something in town. She'd balked at the idea and proposed he simply move back in and stay with her as long as he wanted. As much as he appreciated the offer, he was far too old to be living in his mother's house. That eventually led to her suggestion that he buy the house he'd grown up in. She argued it was more house than she needed anyway, and it would be the perfect size for when he got married and started a family—something she'd been after him to do on and off for a little while now.

Garlic, oregano, and cheese greeted him when he stepped into the kitchen, and he realized just how starving he was. He'd grabbed a burger and fries while waiting around the airport in Nashville but hadn't eaten anything since.

"You've got perfect timing," his sister said as she closed the refrigerator door, two bottles of salad dressing in her hand. "As soon as Tiegan's done with the salad, we can eat."

His niece stood at the counter cutting up mushrooms, and he paused to ruffle her hair. Not surprisingly, his dog, Clifford, sat right by her feet hoping she'd drop some food. The dog ate everything from potato peels and mushrooms to hot dogs and steak. "I'm going to drop my bag off upstairs, and I'll be right back. Is Mom joining us?"

Candace set the lasagna pan on the table and snagged a mushroom off the cutting board when she returned to the counter for the bowl of meatballs. "She's in the basement looking for an old photo album. I have no idea why."

Since his mom had limited space in her apartment, she'd left a lot of sentimental stuff behind in the basement. Considering the amount of stuff she had down there, she might be searching for a long time.

When he'd first moved in, he'd considered using the bedroom he'd grown up in rather than the master bedroom. After all, for as long as he could remember, the room had been his parents'. In the end, he'd decided to make it his own, because it was not only the largest room in the house, but it also had its own bathroom. For the first month or so, he'd slept in his old room while he remodeled the other bedroom and bath. The first thing to go had been the wall-to-wall carpeting, followed by the pea-green paint on the walls. His mom had a thing for the color green. It didn't matter the shade. The master bedroom wasn't the only room painted green; however, the shade in there had been by far the worst. Once done in there, he'd systematically gone through the rest of the house, making changes in every room. Now the place reflected his tastes throughout.

Light spilled out of his niece's bedroom and into the well-lit hallway upstairs. The girl conveniently forgot to switch off lights whenever she left an area. Sometimes during the day, if it was overcast outside, she turned on the lights. When Candace and Tiegan moved in, he'd thought she was just lazy about it, and he'd reminded her every time she did it. Finally, after about two weeks of living with him, she admitted she was afraid of the dark. Now he kept his mouth shut, and unless Tiegan was out of the house, he didn't touch whatever she left on.

The hallway light provided enough illumination for him to leave his suitcase and computer bag just inside his bedroom. Later he'd need to log in to his email and see if he had any issues to tackle, but it could wait until after dinner.

"You're home." His mom closed the basement door behind her as she reentered the kitchen. "How was your flight?"

"Long."

While he disliked air travel because of the inconveniences associated with it, his mom was deathly afraid of it.

"Did you find what you were looking for down there?" Candace asked. Already seated at the kitchen table, she added a slice of lasagna to her plate before reaching for his.

Nodding, Mom held up a photo album with the words *The Elementary Years* printed across the front along with a school picture, possibly kindergarten or first grade, of Elise. He knew somewhere downstairs his mom had similar albums for him and Candace. "Mason needs a picture of Elise when she was in fifth grade for a school project." Mom set the photo album down on the counter by the side door before joining them. "I'm going to scan one and email it to Elise tonight so he can get started, and on Monday, I will mail the whole album out to her. It's hers. She might as well have it."

"I talked to Mason a little while ago. He showed me the picture he's using of Uncle Nick when he was in fifth grade," Tiegan said before stuffing a forkful of food in her mouth.

Born three months apart, his niece and nephew were as close as siblings. And when Elise and her family had lived in New Hampshire, they'd spent as much time together as possible. When his brother-in-law took a position in South Carolina four and a half years ago, it'd been hard on both of them. Thanks to modern technology, they stayed in regular contact with each other, but Aaron knew it wasn't the same.

"Uncle Nick is wearing a tie in the picture," she added once she swallowed the food in her mouth. Like everyone, his niece had plenty of bad habits, but she had excellent table manners.

Shaking her head, Candace added a generous amount of ranch dressing to her salad. "Why doesn't that surprise me?"

He'd had the same thought. His brother-in-law was a great guy, and he'd known him since high school. Nick had moved to Avon right before his freshman year and started dating Elise not long after. But in a lot of ways, Nick had been born in the wrong decade. He was perhaps the only person Aaron knew who'd never shown up at school in jeans.

His niece took control of the conversation for the next several minutes. First, she filled him in on what she'd been up to at school. Oddly enough, Tiegan had the same fifth grade teacher he'd had at Avon Elementary, and she loved her. For the most part, Tiegan loved school, and she got upset whenever she didn't get a perfect grade on an assignment. Although she and her cousin had a lot in common, when it came to school, they were at opposite ends of the spectrum. His nephew did what he needed for school and then dismissed it from his mind. In fact, not once while he'd been at Elise's house had Mason mentioned school to him. Instead, many of their conversations had been about either sports— Mason played on a sports team in every season—or his favorite new video game. Once Tiegan exhausted the topic of school, she gave him the 411 on the birthday party she'd gone to the previous weekend.

"Wow. An indoor skydiving place." When he'd been a kid, his birthday parties had been either at the house or Skate Kingdom, a roller-skating rink that was no longer in business. His sisters' parties had been similar. "Where is it?" He knew every business in town, and an indoor skydiving place was not among them. Not to mention, such a place probably wouldn't survive in Avon.

"North Conway. It opened about three months ago. They offer indoor surfing too. It's part of a chain. There is one in Nashua and a few in Massachusetts, as well as one in Connecticut. The owners are probably hoping it'll be a big draw for the tourists," his sister answered.

If it was going to succeed this far north, then the North Conway area made the most sense. In the winter, skiers flocked to the area, and in the summer and fall, vacationers descended on the vicinity.

Candace's mention of tourists brought to mind the one who'd rented all five cottages the previous weekend. "Any issues with your guest, Mom?"

Countless times over the years, wealthy individuals from

places like Weston or Boston came to the lake to "rough it," as if staying in a cottage with running water and electricity was somehow roughing it. Often, but not always, these guests made the worst customers. And a person didn't get much wealthier than Juliette Belmont.

To say it had shocked him when his mom shared their guest's identity would be perhaps the greatest understatement of the century. When he'd received the text message, he'd read it twice before replying and asking if she was possibly talking about someone else who happened to share the same name. He'd had a classmate named Selena Cruise in college, and she hadn't been the well-known actress. In her reply, his mom confirmed she'd shown the billionaire cover model to cottage number ten.

"Nope. She's been a great guest so far."

He hoped it stayed that way. "Any idea why she picked here?"

The woman's family owned a hotel chain, not to mention she had enough money to travel anywhere in the world she wanted. As much as he loved his little corner of the globe, it didn't compare to the places someone like Juliette Belmont could and probably did visit on a regular basis.

"Do you remember Holly Lambert?"

Even if Holly wasn't the most famous person to ever come out of Avon, he'd remember her. The schools in town consisted of slightly more students now thanks to a recent increase in population, but when he'd been a student, each grade had consisted of about a hundred kids. Holly had been two grades below him all the way through school, and she'd been friends with Candace.

"Yeah, of course."

"She and Holly are good friends. Holly recommended she stay with us. And the day Juliette checked in, Holly was with her."

Well, that answered one question. "But why did she come here?"

"I didn't ask her, and she didn't share. But she doesn't want a lot of people to know she's here."

Across the table, his sister cut another piece of lasagna and added it to her plate before looking at him. "Do you want more?"

Rather than answer, he handed over his plate.

"Tiegan and I ran into her on Thursday when we were out walking. We saw her again this morning. I like her. She reminds me a little of Holly." His sister handed him back his plate before picking up her daughter's and giving her a second helping of lasagna as well.

If any other almost eleven-year-old knew someone like Juliette was staying in town, he'd worry that everyone in Avon would soon know too. But when it came to keeping secrets, Tiegan was a vault. Last year they'd planned a large surprise birthday party for his mom. Even though Tiegan had been seeing her grandmother several times a week at the time, she never said a word. And at Christmastime she'd kept her lips sealed even though she'd known Elise, Nick, and Mason were coming for the holiday so her grandmother would be surprised when she came over on Christmas morning and found everyone gathered together. If word got out that Juliette was staying at one of their cottages, it wouldn't be because Tiegan told someone.

"She's going to come over for dinner on Tuesday night."

He didn't mind visitors, and he'd told Candace to treat this as her own house when she moved in. Still, the individual in cottage number ten was one dinner guest he'd rather not have.

"You don't mind, do you?" his sister asked, as if picking up on his thoughts.

Aaron shook his head. "You're free to invite anyone you want over, Candace. I told you that before."

JULIETTE PULLED up the weather app on her phone while she finished her hot tea, even though she doubted it would change her mind. Except for Wednesday, she'd gone for a walk every day since she'd arrived. And rain, not the temperature, was the only reason she'd skipped it then. While she didn't mind the rain on a hot summer afternoon, the temperature on Wednesday had been hovering around forty degrees—a tad too chilly to get soaked while taking an afternoon stroll.

Since the Wrights owned a significant chunk of land and much of it remained untouched, she'd explored a different area each day. Sometimes her walks brought her past the other cottages. Other times her walks brought her through the woods. She'd never done any hiking, and she'd always considered herself a city lover. Yet she thoroughly enjoyed her solitary outings where, except for her brief meetings with Candace and her daughter, the only other life she saw was the occasional chipmunk or squirrel. In fact, with each passing day, she wondered if perhaps she should purchase a vacation home in a place like Avon for those times in the future when she wanted a break from the city.

"Forty-three degrees." While three degrees warmer than yesterday, she wouldn't be breaking out her shorts anytime soon. However, she would be making use of her new gloves and hat. And when she got back home, she'd probably once again indulge in a large mug of hot chocolate. She hadn't added cocoa mix to the list of items she gave Mrs. Lambert, but she was glad the woman had thought to buy some for her. It wasn't the only extra item she'd come across when she put away the food Holly's mom picked up last weekend. There'd also been a package of chocolate chip cookies, a jar of peanut butter, and one of marshmallow fluff. So far, the cocoa powder was the only thing she'd indulged in. But every time she opened the cabinet and spotted the two jars, her craving for a peanut butter and fluff sandwich—or a fluffernutter, as they called it in New England—grew.

She managed to get her boots and jacket on before the ringing cell phone in her pocket forced her to put her walk on hold. While she'd received countless calls since she arrived, she'd only answered a handful of them. The last one had been on Thursday when Holly called to let her know she was headed to Maine and to pass along her mom's message that if Juliette needed anything to just call or text her. Considering the amount of food in her fridge, she shouldn't need anything for at least another week.

The name Curt appeared on the device now. She hadn't spoken to her cousin since her sister's wedding. Actually, he was the only one of her first cousins she hadn't talked to since the media started running the stories about her and Daniel's relationship. She'd known it was only a matter of time before he reached out as well.

Dropping her gloves on the table, she answered the phone.

"Sorry I didn't call sooner. We just got home yesterday," Curt said after greeting her.

That explained why she hadn't heard from Curt until now. With everything else, she'd forgotten Curt, Taylor, his fiancée, and Taylor's niece had flown down to Florida the day after Courtney's wedding.

"How are you doing?" he asked.

Annoyed. Angry. "Okay." She kept the other adjectives to herself because complaining didn't change anything.

"Leah told me you're hanging out in my neck of the woods."

She considered her cousin Leah one of her closest friends. When she'd decided to retreat up here for an extended vacation, she'd been one of the first people Juliette let know. She wasn't surprised Leah had passed the information on to her older brother.

If she had to guess, she'd say Pelham was about two hours away from Avon. In her opinion, that wasn't precisely Curt's neck of the woods, but she wasn't going to correct him. "I got here last weekend."

"Leah said you're staying in Avon. I was up that way in October. How do you like it?"

"A bit more rural than I expected, but I like it. It's quiet."

Before Curt left Nichols Investment and moved to New Hampshire to focus on his writing career, he'd lived in Boston, so he knew well how much life in a small town differed from living in the city.

"The media doesn't know you're there?"

"I don't think so. And if it does, no one has bothered me."

"Glad to hear it. If you want some company, I can drive up either this week or next."

As much as she loved the solitude, she wouldn't mind a short visit from Curt or any of her cousins, assuming they didn't spend the night. Her parents were a different matter. "Sounds good. Whenever you have the time. I'll text you the address of where I'm staying. I'm warning you, though, the town isn't big on street signs." If and when she ventured out, she'd probably need her GPS to find her way back to the cottage. "So, how was your trip?"

By the time Curt finished telling her about his vacation and all the fun the three of them had at the theme parks in Florida, she wanted to go herself. The enormous crowds she'd encounter kept her from making any plans to visit in the near future.

"Taylor and Reese are expecting me, so I need to go, but

I'll see you later in the week. If you need me to bring you anything, let me know."

"Will do. And say hi to Taylor and Reese for me." Ending the call, Juliette stuck the cell phone back in her jacket pocket and pulled on her gloves.

Cold air and silence greeted her when she stepped outside. For a moment, she stood on the little front porch and let both wash over her while enjoying the lake view. While it hadn't been his intention, her conversation with Curt had conjured up thoughts of the stories circulating about her and the fact she'd dated a married man. And yes, they were still going around. She'd made the mistake of checking the *Star Insider's* website last night. Some of the pictures posted were ones she'd never seen. But one stood out from the rest. It'd been of a man and a woman in bed. Since some of the pictures of her and Daniel had been taken together inside his home, she assumed the couple was in his bedroom, but because she'd never stepped foot in his room, she wasn't positive. While all you could see was the woman's naked back, she had blonde hair about the same length as Juliette's, so the site was claiming she was the woman in the photo. However, it wasn't possible, because they'd been at her place the one time they'd been intimate.

As she stood outside, though, thoughts of the media and the photo disappeared. It wasn't the first time since she'd been at the cottage that she'd stood in the same spot and whatever concerns she had drifted away, proving she'd made the right decision in coming here.

Her first instinct was to walk along the perimeter of the lake, but at the last minute, she pulled out the map of the campground Mrs. Wright left her when she checked in. She'd already put a little checkmark next to the various paths she'd explored, but there were several left. One in particular caught her eye now. To reach it, she needed to follow the edge of the lake until she reached the area near cottage number twenty. At least by the looks of it, the path into the woods started somewhere behind the building and ended closer to the campground's office. And unlike the streets in town, all the trails she'd followed so far had been well marked, suggesting the Wrights didn't want guests getting lost on their property.

With a route decided upon, Juliette returned the map to the safety of her pocket and set off. A slight breeze blew the few pieces of hair not under her hat in her eyes, and she brushed them aside. Today, like every day this week, the lake remained empty, a large portion of it still covered by ice. Exactly how thick the ice was, she didn't know, and she didn't care to determine by stepping on it and finding herself submerged in icy water. Despite the lack of activity now, Holly assured her Avon Lake was a favorite of ice fishermen and skaters in January and February, and a hub of boating activity started around Memorial Day weekend, more or less around the time she'd be getting ready to leave. However, Juliette didn't know where she'd go. She always had her place in Manhattan, but depending on what other changes she decided to make, it might not be the most optimal location. And if she chose to accept her mom's offer to work at the Helping Hands Foundation, she'd have to move closer to Rhode Island. A relocation to Providence or Newport would allow her to be closer to much of her family, especially her sister, who she'd learned this week was pregnant. At the same time, though, if she returned to New York, she'd be closer to her brother and his family.

"First you need to figure out what you want to do."

Wednesday afternoon, Pierre, her agent, had called wanting to know when she'd be back in the city and whether or not she wanted to be part of the Jolie fall fashion show again. She'd been part of every one of its shows since the former pop singer turned designer launched her label. Unlike some of the bigger ones in New York and Paris, the label's shows had a whole different kind of energy while at the same time being far less stressful. Regardless, she wasn't sure she wanted to participate in this new fall launch, especially considering she didn't care for the latest style Jolie had adopted. Needless to say, when she told Pierre she'd get back to him, he hadn't been happy.

Honestly, she didn't care if he was happy or not.

Spotting cottage number twenty up ahead, she headed for the large gap separating the building from its neighbor. Just as the map indicated, the entrance to the path was a short distance from the house. Unlike while walking along the lake, here trees closed in around her. At the moment, their limbs remained bare, but leaves would create a canopy of shade in another two months or so. She looked forward to seeing it.

The phone in her pocket rang, the sound unusually loud in the silence. Pulling it out, she checked the caller ID. Rather than the name of a family member or friend, there was only a phone number—one she didn't know, although she recognized the 212 area code. The only people in New York she'd take a call from were in her contact list. Whoever was calling now could leave her a message, and depending on who it was, she'd call them back later.

One minute she was walking with her finger about to press the decline icon, and the next she was flailing her arms like a bird trying to take off. Pain shot through her knee when it made contact with a rock. Instinctively, she put her hands out to help break her fall, dropping her phone and the glove she'd removed in the process.

"Ugh." Slowly, she moved into a sitting position as she waited for the pain in her knee and the stinging in her palm to subside. No doubt, when she looked later, she'd find a nice bruise on her knee. "That's what I get for not paying attention."

She'd been talking to herself an awful lot the past day or two. She guessed it was a side effect of spending so much time alone, something she wasn't at all used to.

Snap. A jingling sound followed the first noise. Until now, the only sounds around her other than her ringing cell phone had been the occasional rustle of dead leaves caused by a chipmunk or a squirrel scurrying across the ground. Neither animal was heavy enough to snap twigs, and unless they'd started wearing jewelry, they couldn't be the cause of the jingling either.

The cause of the new sounds came into view as she retrieved her phone and glove. She'd met Clifford yesterday. The dog had been with Candace and her daughter when she saw them while out walking. The man jogging with Clifford, she'd never met, but thanks to Holly's description and the fact the property belonged to the Wrights, she assumed the guy headed her way was Aaron. And she understood why her friend had had a thing for him while in high school. He looked about the same height as her brother, who was an inch over six feet. A black long-sleeved base layer shirt hugged his broad shoulders and emphasized his flat abdomen. A black beanie covered his head, but his short and sexy beard told her his hair was dark like his sister's. Even from a distance, his arresting good looks captured her full attention, and with no trouble, she could see him starring alongside Anderson Brady or her sister's husband in a summer blockbuster.

Slowly, she came to her feet and watched the muscles rippling under his shirt as he approached her. She didn't know if the man was single or not, but if he was, the women in Avon must be blind.

He could be a total creep. She'd met plenty of gorgeous men who turned out to be the biggest jerks in the world.

Clifford reached her first and stopped, but his owner wasn't far behind.

Green. The dog's owner possessed the most beautiful green eyes. She rarely associated the word beautiful with a man, but she didn't know how else to describe his eyes.

"Are you okay?" he asked, his voice deep and oh so sensual, sending a ripple of awareness through her, and she forgot about the throbbing in her knee.

CHAPTER 4

WHENEVER POSSIBLE, Aaron preferred to run outside rather than on the treadmill in his basement. While he occasionally ran the streets in town, especially during the peak months when every cottage was rented out, as a former cross-country runner in high school and college, he preferred to use the trails through the woods. When he and Clifford set out this morning, he hadn't expected them to come across anything but a few squirrels and maybe a bird or two. Never in a million years had he thought he'd find the campground's only occupant on her knees in the middle of the woods. But when he'd come around the corner, there she'd been, and now she stood a few feet away scratching Clifford behind the ears. Not surprisingly, the dog was basking in the attention. If he loved anything more than food, it was a good scratch behind the ears or a belly rub.

Juliette gave Clifford one final scratch before pulling her glove back on. Why it was off in the first place, he didn't know. "I'm fine."

He gave her a quick once-over before settling his eyes on her face. Damn, he'd been wrong. The various magazines hadn't photoshopped her photos before using them on their covers. Her face was simply as perfect as it appeared in those photos. And her eyes, well he'd assumed the color had been digitally enhanced because he'd never met anyone with eyes so blue they bordered on sapphire. Clearly, though, photo manipulation had nothing to do with their color.

"I tripped. It's what I get for not paying attention. I'm Juliette, by the way. Are you Candace's brother, Aaron?"

At the sound of his name, his manners returned, and he realized he hadn't introduced himself. "Sorry. Yes." He extended his gloved hand, half expecting Juliette not to take it. People with money could be weird. "Are you sure you're okay?" The last thing his mother needed was Juliette suing her because she injured herself while on the property.

Shaking his hand, she nodded. "I'll probably have a bruise on my knee, but yeah, I'm fine."

"Then I'll let you get back to your walk. Enjoy."

Regardless of how gorgeous the woman before him was, he didn't have time to stand around and talk. He needed to finish up his run and shower. His sister had a lot of studying to do, so he'd promised to take Tiegan to the movies and lunch so Candace could have the house to herself. The theater was showing the new superhero movie Tiegan wanted to see at noon but not again until eight. If they missed the afternoon show, they'd have to drive over to the theater in North Conway, which he'd rather not do today. He'd spent enough time traveling yesterday.

Juliette smiled, and a jolt of awareness hit him hard, reminding him just how long it'd been since he'd had sex. Hell, never mind had sex, it'd been longer than he cared to admit since he even went out with a woman. As much as he loved living in Avon, its limited population of single women his age made dating difficult.

"You too. I'll see you on Tuesday night."

42

He'd been thinking about being conveniently absent for dinner that night. "See you then."

Aaron watched her walk away. Her oversized ski jacket concealed her figure from the hips up. His eyes dropped lower to her jeans-clad legs. Man, the things went on forever. It shouldn't surprise him. The woman was a model. As far as he knew, models were never short. Although why, he didn't know. Women came in all different shapes and sizes, so at least to him, it didn't make sense that you never saw a five-foot-tall woman showing off clothes for the top designers.

Before he could stop himself, he conjured up an image of Juliette in a far different outfit, and his damn body once again reminded him exactly how long he'd been alone. "I need to get out more, Clifford." Reaching down, he scratched the dog near his collar, then started running again.

OPENING the door to the theater, Aaron waited for his niece to exit. He'd been watching movies at the Palladium Theater on Main Street his entire life. From the outside, it resembled an old-school movie theater. Aaron doubted the building's exterior appearance had changed since the theater first opened decades ago. However, the same couldn't be said about the interior. Like its larger counterparts, the theater had the latest audio and visual technology and heated seats. He never used the option, but his mom, who always found the theater too cold, used it whenever she went. The Palladium also had the best popcorn around.

"What did you think of the movie?" Rather than head toward the parking lot and his car, they started down the sidewalk toward George's Diner. Unlike the movie theater, both the interior and exterior of the establishment appeared part of a different time—not that it seemed to hurt business. The place was rarely empty.

Tiegan kicked a small rock on the sidewalk as they walked. "It was good, but I think I liked the first one better."

Designed as a trio, the first of the series had come out the previous summer. The last installment was due out in the fall, and he was anxious to see how the writers tied up all the loose ends. "Me too."

The Beatles' song "Twist and Shout" greeted them when he pulled open the diner's door. While the food was delicious, and you'd find everything from burgers and fries to vegan and gluten-free options on the menu, you would not find any modern music at George's.

Today, like any other Sunday afternoon, people occupied roughly half the booths and tables. Several customers also sat at the counter. Unlike many restaurants in the city, there was no hostess waiting to seat you when you walked in. Instead, if you saw an empty table, you took it.

He picked a booth near the door and grabbed two of the menus placed at the end of the table. "What do you think you're going to get to eat?"

"Either fried chicken or a mushroom cheeseburger." She opened her menu, then looked up at him. "Can I get a milkshake?"

His sister made sure Tiegan ate healthy at home, so one milkshake with him wouldn't make a difference—besides, it wasn't like his niece sat around on the couch all day eating potato chips and playing video games. She might not participate in as many sports as his nephew, but the girl was constantly on the go, either dancing around the house or riding her bike outside.

"Go for it."

He was deciding whether to have a steak and onion sub or a bacon double cheeseburger when Christine Cote, someone he'd graduated high school with and the owner's daughter, approached their table, notepad in hand ready to take their order.

While Christine's mom owned the diner, her grandparents had actually opened it back in the 1950s. And although her mom still played a role in the business, Christine oversaw many of the day-to-day operations, and everyone in town knew it was only a matter of time before the older woman turned the reins over to her completely.

"Hi, Aaron," she greeted. "I haven't seen you in weeks. How have you been?"

They'd never dated, although during freshman year he'd wanted to ask her out. Unfortunately, Dwayne Cote got to her first. However, they had run cross-country together all four years of high school and gone to the prom together as friends their junior year.

"Good. How is everyone?" Although Christine and Dwayne broke up for a short time during junior year, they'd gotten back together the summer before senior year. They'd been together ever since and now had two children, a son Tiegan's age and a two-year-old daughter.

"Oh, everyone's fine. Are you two ready to order?"

Tiegan spoke up before he could answer. "Can I have a mushroom cheeseburger with onion rings instead of french fries and a chocolate milkshake with whipped cream?"

Christine glanced at him as if to ask if it was okay for her to order that, and he nodded. His niece had stopped ordering off the children's menu a long time ago.

"I'll be right back with your drinks," she promised after he ordered a bacon double cheeseburger and a vanilla milkshake. He'd planned to get an iced coffee, but as soon as his niece mentioned a milkshake, he'd started craving one too.

No longer needing it, Tiegan returned her menu to the holder on the table and turned her eyes on him. While she resembled his sister considerably, she had her father's eyes—a man he'd love to hunt down and beat some sense into. Even after almost a year, Aaron found it impossible to comprehend how Eric could just up and walk out not only on his wife but also on his daughter. Perhaps even worse was the fact he didn't bother to stay in contact with Tiegan. Aaron could count on one hand the number of times Eric had reached out to her since he left town.

"Is there anything else you want to do before we head home?" He enjoyed spending time with his niece, but it wasn't the only reason he was asking. The way he saw it, the longer he kept Tiegan out of the house, the longer his sister could study without any interruptions.

She didn't hesitate to reply. "Can we go shopping for some new clothes?"

Aaron didn't have any objection to spending money on his niece. But he did have an objection to stepping foot in the mall. Even when he needed to purchase items for himself, he tried to do so on the internet rather than venture to the mall. "You should probably go shopping with your mom or Nana."

"Yeah, I guess. You don't know anything about girls' clothes." She propped her chin on her hand. "When we get home, can we take Clifford for a walk?"

Even before Candace and Tiegan moved in, his niece and Clifford had been best buds. Now they were practically inseparable. The dog even slept in her room every night. And while he recognized she was far more mature than most children a few weeks shy of eleven, both he and Candace had agreed she needed to have an adult with her if she took Clifford for a walk in the woods.

His niece's words conjured up the image of Juliette smiling this morning, but he pushed it aside because the last person he needed occupying his thoughts was her. "If you want."

Christine returned with a milkshake in each hand. "Here you go, Tiegan." She placed the chocolate concoction down near his niece before setting his vanilla one down. "Did you hear Holly Lambert is in town? Or at least she was. She came in on Wednesday with her mom for lunch. It was the first time I've seen her in at least two years."

Aaron's thoughts immediately returned to the other celebrity currently in Avon. No questions about it, Juliette Belmont was the most beautiful woman he'd ever met. "My mom mentioned she saw her last week." Christine didn't need to know where or with whom Holly had been with at the time.

"She looked fantastic. But of course, she probably has a personal trainer and nutritionist telling her exactly what to do."

What was the proper reply to that? Especially since there wasn't anything wrong with the way Christine looked. Sure, she appeared a little tired, but she worked full-time and had two kids, so that wasn't surprising.

"Well, Mrs. Lambert seemed happy. I know she wishes Holly would come home more."

His mom said the same thing about his sister Elise. He imagined having children—regardless of their age—who lived more than an hour or two from home could be tough on parents.

"Christine, can I get another coffee?" the older gentleman with his wife at the next table asked, putting a temporary halt to their conversation.

"Sure thing, Martin," she replied before looking back at Aaron. "I'll talk to you later."

"Who's Holly Lambert?" Tiegan asked.

One thing he'd learned since she and Candace moved in with him was that the girl hated to be left in the dark. It didn't matter the topic or the situation.

"Just someone your mom and I went to school with. I think she lives in New York City now." Honestly, he didn't know, and he didn't care, because where she lived didn't affect his life in any way.

"Nana said Juliette is from New York City."

Considering who she was and what she did for a living, that made sense, though much like with Holly, he didn't care.

"I really want to go to New York. I'd love to see the Rockettes or the New York City ballet. Do you know it's one of the best dance companies in the world? I read a book about it for my nonfiction book report." While Tiegan enjoyed playing basketball and softball, her real passion was dance. Unfortunately, at the moment she wasn't able to take any classes.

"You don't have to go to New York to see the ballet. There's a professional ballet company in Boston. If you want, I can see if they are performing anything you might like and get you and your mom tickets for your birthday."

Tiegan nodded, a grin stretching across her face. "That would be awesome. Can you and Nana come too?"

If she wanted to see a basketball or baseball game, he'd tag along in a heartbeat. Hell, he'd take her himself. Ballets were another story. He attended a performance of *The Nutcracker* while living in Boston because a woman he'd been dating at the time loved the ballet. He had no desire to see another show. At the same time, he hated disappointing the girl across the table from him. "We'll see."

JULIETTE STOPPED at the thermostat on her way to the sofa and turned up the heat. She tended to keep the temperature set somewhere between sixty-eight and seventy at home. The temperature inside right now was nowhere near that. Before sitting down, she glanced at the woodstove. Maybe she should call Valley Landscaping and have them deliver some wood so she could use the thing. She could give them her credit card info over the phone, and they could leave the wood outside. How hard could it be to carry in a few pieces when she needed them?

"Oh, yeah, great idea. I'll probably burn the cottage down trying to get a fire going."

Talk about a fabulous way to call attention to herself. She could picture the headlines already on *Today Magazine* or the *Star Report*. Juliette Belmont, President Warren Sherbrooke's niece, destroys home owned by Maggie Wright, a lifelong resident of Avon, New Hampshire. Knowing her luck, she'd not only burn down this cottage but all the ones around her too. Yeah, it was safer to leave the woodstove alone and simply rely on the central heating, even if it wasn't as efficient as she'd like.

Kicking off her sneakers, she grabbed her e-reader off the end table. Her cousin's second novel was due out in November, and she still hadn't read his first one. As far as she knew, she was the only member of the family who hadn't read *Fatal Deception*. It wasn't that she didn't want to support Curt, but from the little she knew about the book, it wasn't her type of story. She enjoyed books with either a lot of humor or a happily ever after. Novels filled with plot twists and turns or crazed psychopaths didn't appeal to her. Regardless, she planned to read it before she started anything else, and now seemed as good a time as any to start.

She flipped open the cover and pressed the power button before taking a sip of her hot chocolate. "Okay, Curt, let's see why everyone thinks this book is so great."

Her cousin's book had hit all the major lists, and both Curt's fans and family members were clamoring for its sequel. Adjusting the pillow behind her back, she winced when she drew her knees up in front of her. As she'd expected, she had an enormous bruise on her knee from when she tripped. The way she saw it, a bruise was far better than a sprained ankle or a broken bone. Next time she went walking through the woods, she needed to be more careful. She'd had her fair share of both when she danced, and she had no desire to experience either again. Hot chocolate in one hand, she dove into the story.

Five chapters later, Juliette understood why so many people loved *Fatal Deception*. Never in a million years would she have guessed her cousin was such a talented storyteller. In her opinion, he'd wasted way too many years in Boston working in the financial world. Setting her e-reader down, she rubbed her eyes as she stood and then stretched her arms over her head. After she grabbed something to eat and another hot drink, she'd get back to the book.

Despite her empty stomach, movement outside had her walking toward the windows rather than the kitchen.

Aaron and Tiegan were walking his dog along the lake. Unlike earlier, he had on a dark blue ski jacket and jeans. Not that it mattered. She could easily picture the way his muscles had moved as he ran this morning. The man took care of himself. The last thing she needed right now was to get involved with anyone, especially since her stay in Avon was temporary. Still, it didn't mean she couldn't look and appreciate a man. And at least in the looks department, there was a lot to appreciate when it came to Mr. Aaron Wright.

Her eyes lingered on him for another second or two before moving over to Tiegan, who at the moment was talking and making hand gestures as her uncle listened. The girl was, in a single word, striking. Juliette didn't know what her dad looked like, but considering how attractive the few members of her family she'd met were, it wasn't a big surprise. Without any trouble, Juliette could see the girl doing photoshoots for the biggest names in pre-teen clothing or walking the runway during New York Fashion Week.

When she joined the family for dinner, maybe she'd offer to put Tiegan in contact with her agent, assuming the girl was interested and Candace approved—something the woman might not do. Her parents had refused to let her pursue that particular goal until she was seventeen. In fact, it was the only thing she could remember her parents ever refusing to let her try as a kid. But if Candace gave the okay, there wasn't anyone better to represent Tiegan than Pierre. As annoying as he could be at times, the man knew the business inside and out. More importantly, he looked at the talent he represented as more than just a commodity he could use to make money. Not to mention, he was always on the lookout for the next breakout model, a title she believed Tiegan could easily earn.

Before they disappeared from view, she glanced back at Aaron. Yep, she could spend a lot of time appreciating Mr. Wright.

Juliette stayed by the window until she could no longer see Aaron and his niece. Was the man single? Holly might know, and if she didn't, she could find out from her mom. According to Holly, in Avon everyone knew everyone else's business, and secrets never stayed that way for long.

And what if he is? She'd come here to escape the media, which she'd done so far, and make some decisions about her life—a task she was still working on. Neither of those things required a man. It was probably in her best interest to maintain a look-but-don't-touch attitude when it came to the campground owner's son. Or anyone else in town, for that matter.

Despite telling herself not to worry about Aaron's relationship status and simply appreciate him from afar, she found herself pulling up Holly's contact information in her phone instead of picking up her e-reader again when she finished lunch half an hour later.

Holly answered on the third ring. "I was thinking about calling you today. How are things?"

"Okay. Are you still in Maine with your cousin?"

"Yeah, I plan to stay for a few more days, and then I'm going to head back to Avon."

She'd expected Holly to return to New York after seeing her cousin. "Really? You're not going back to the city?"

"Nah, I'm staying with my parents for another week or so. Before I left for Maine, Marc told me he plans to propose to his girlfriend. He already bought the ring."

She'd last seen Marc in late October when he came to visit Holly. At the time, he'd come alone, and she didn't remember him mentioning a girlfriend. She didn't recall Holly telling her Marc had a girlfriend either. "I didn't know he was seeing anyone."

"Neither did I. I can't believe he never told me. I'm his twin, for crying out loud."

Juliette didn't tell her siblings about every man she dated. Then again, few of her relationships ever lasted more than a month or two. But if one did or if she was with someone she thought she might have a future with, she made sure everyone in her family met him. "How long have they been together?"

"Since January. They haven't even been together for three months, and he's going to propose. It's crazy. And trust me, I told him that."

Oh, Juliette didn't doubt it. When it came to sharing what was on her mind, Holly held nothing back. Her twin seemed to be the same way. At least that had always been the case when she'd been around Marc.

"Just because he bought a ring doesn't mean he plans to ask this month."

Holly laughed. "You know my brother. The guy has the

patience of a two-year-old. He'll ask before the month is over. Convincing him to wait until they've been together longer will never happen. So I'm going to spend some more time in town and get to know her."

As interesting as their conversation was, she hadn't called to hear about Holly's brother and his engagement plans. "Speaking of meeting someone, I met your high school crush this morning."

"I haven't seen him in at least two years. Please tell me he's still panty-melting hot. And if he has a beer belly and no hair, just lie to me."

Juliette adjusted her position on the couch, grimacing a little when she stretched her bruised leg out straight. "Your panties would be sufficiently melted if you saw him." She wasn't lying. The man had most definitely caught her attention both times she'd seen him. "It's kind of why I called. Do you know if he's single?" His sister and niece lived with him, which made her think he wasn't married, but it didn't rule out anything else.

"No clue. But I can find out. I'm sure my mom or sister knows. Do you want me to call them?"

"Nah, don't worry about it. I was just curious." Until the media moved on to something other than her and Daniel, it was probably best she didn't get into another relationship.

"Curious or bored?"

Except for her walks, she hadn't left the cottage, so she should be bored, because it wasn't like her to sit around at home for days and days. Oddly, boredom hadn't struck her once.

"Instead of bored, maybe I should have asked if you're lonely and looking for someone to pass the time with while you're there. And if Aaron looks as good as the last time I saw him, I don't blame you for wanting to spend your lonely nights with him."

Despite the lack of company, she hadn't been lonely since she'd checked in. "Curious. Until pictures of Daniel and me stop popping up everywhere, I think it's better I don't get involved with anyone." Heaven knew how they might drag someone she started spending time with into the little drama.

"It might be a while before that happens. But if you change your mind, I can get you an answer in a matter of minutes."

Thanks for the reminder.

"Have you checked the *Star Report* website recently?"

Juliette groaned. "Before you even ask, that's not me and Daniel having sex. He must have been seeing someone besides me." If he'd been getting some from another woman, it explained why he'd been willing to wait as long as he had to sleep with her.

"I had a feeling it wasn't you. The woman's hair looked longer than yours."

Most people, including her parents, if they ever saw the picture—man, she hoped they didn't—wouldn't look close enough to notice the difference in hair length.

"Daniel was more of a jerk than I thought. I hope his wife takes him to the cleaners." An annoying beep followed Holly's statement, signaling that someone was trying to reach one of them. "It's my mom," Holly said before Juliette checked her phone. "I'm going to ask her about Aaron in case you change your mind. And if you see him again, tell him I said hello."

Telling Holly not to bother was a waste of time, so she didn't comment on Holly's statement. "Talk to you later."

CHAPTER 5

JULIETTE STARTED her day with a long walk first along the lake and then the same path she'd followed yesterday. Despite her constant reminders to herself that getting into any kind of relationship while up here was a bad idea, she kept a lookout for Aaron. Unfortunately, the only life she saw came in the form of a single chipmunk. Man, those buggers moved quickly when startled.

Although she hadn't been able to visually appreciate the man again, thanks to Mrs. Lambert, she learned a boatload about him when Holly called her back. In fact, when it came to details about Aaron, Mrs. Lambert put the internet and all its search engines to shame.

According to Holly's mom, not only was Aaron unmarried as she'd assumed, but he wasn't seeing anyone, much to his mother's dismay. During their conversation, Mrs. Lambert shared with Holly that Aaron's mom often mentioned how much she hoped her son would get married and start a family.

Aaron's current relationship status wasn't the only detail she'd learned about him either, thanks to Holly and her mom. She also now knew he worked for a company in Boston. Mrs.

Lambert couldn't remember its name, but she knew he did something with computers there. Whatever it was, though, he worked from home most of the time and traveled into the city a few times a month. While giving Holly those bites of information, she'd shared that his niece and sister had moved in with him about seven months ago. However, she didn't have all the details of why Mrs. Lambert assumed the move was related to Candace's divorce last summer.

Following her informative conversation with Holly, Juliette left the campground for the first time since she'd arrived. With no destination in mind, she'd left her GPS turned off and simply driven around town. During her wandering, she'd found herself back on Main street. Unlike the day she arrived, the parking lots at each of the schools were full, and students ran around the playground next to one of the buildings. Rather than turn when she reached the four-way intersection on Main Street like she had the previous weekend, she continued straight and found some of the other business Holly had mentioned were scattered around town. After more than an hour of aimless driving, she reached a sign welcoming her to the town of Ashford. Instead of continuing, she pulled over and put the address for the campground into her GPS. Although she'd paid attention to her surroundings while driving, she'd known she'd never make it back to the cottage without assistance. Maybe after a few more trips, she could do it, but not today.

Despite the lack of street signs and one missed turn, she made it back to the campground just as the sky opened up. She'd expected it. Not only had the sky been overcast since she woke up, but the weather app on her phone had said there was a 90 percent chance of rain starting at noon. Still, when the first onslaught of water hit the windshield, she'd sworn. She'd hoped to sit on the porch swing and do some more reading before the rain started because the temperature was a good fifteen degrees warmer than yesterday. Instead, she'd dashed inside before she got soaked. She then proceeded to spend her time first reading and then searching various real estate websites for homes in and around the area. It might be crazy, but she couldn't shake the idea of buying a house either in town or the general area for those weeks when she wanted to get away from the city. But as far as nutty ideas went, it wasn't the worst one she'd ever had. And she could guarantee it wouldn't be the last crazy notion she got either. After all, what fun was it always doing only things that made sense?

The afternoon was long gone now, and her unhappy stomach kept reminding her she'd only had a fruit salad for lunch. While she'd intended to walk up to the Wrights' house for dinner, the rain forced her to nix her plan and drive instead.

Candace opened the door before Juliette rang the door-bell. "Come on in before you get soaked. Unless you're a duck, this has been a pretty miserable day."

She didn't hesitate to step inside. "It could be worse. It could be snowing." When she wanted to ski, she liked the cold, wet stuff, but at all other times, she found it a plain nuisance.

"I'd rather have it snow any day," Candace said as she closed and locked the front door. "If you want to give me your jacket, I'll hang it up for you."

She'd thought about not wearing it—it wasn't like she was going to be spending time outside. In the end, she'd pulled it on to keep from getting wet to and from the car.

"The potatoes need about another ten minutes in the oven." Her hostess hung Juliette's jacket in the large hall closet. "I should have asked when I invited you if you were a vegetarian or allergic to any foods. It didn't occur to me until I took the roast out of the oven."

Juliette had attempted a vegetarian diet when she was

about thirteen. She'd made it three months before her cravings for hamburgers and sausage pizza had her calling it quits. While she ate a lot of fresh fruits and vegetables and very little sausage pizza these days, there wasn't any type of food that she eliminated from her diet. "No allergies, and I'll eat almost anything except lamb." Some people might love it, but she couldn't stand even its smell, never mind the taste.

Candace wrinkled her nose. "My brother likes it, but I don't know how anyone eats lamb."

Juliette followed her hostess down the hall and into a large open kitchen. Light gray cabinets occupied one of the walls while two large sliding glass doors led out to a massive deck. Several barstools were positioned near a portion of the counter. A table set for five was near the glass doors, allowing diners to eat while enjoying the view of the lake. Other than some small potted plants on the windowsill over the sink, there were no personal touches or pictures in the room.

"Can I get you a drink? I was going to open some wine, but if you'd rather have something else, I made some iced tea earlier. I can also make you a cup of coffee."

Unsure of what to do with herself, Juliette pulled out a barstool and sat. "Whatever you're having is fine."

Candace removed a box of wine from the small built-in wine fridge, a feature Juliette didn't think was original to the house. After pouring two glasses, she handed Juliette one before taking a sip of hers. "I expect my mom and Tiegan any second. After school today, Tiegan went over there to work on a school project. Mom's the arts and crafts guru of the family."

Well, that explained the absence of two people but unfortunately not the one she was most interested in seeing tonight.

"I used to hate school projects." She'd always preferred exams and quizzes to projects that required hours upon hours of work.

"Me too. Tiegan's teacher loves them. She seems to have one every other week. Personally, I think she gives so many because they're easy to grade."

Juliette had never thought about it, but Candace made a good point. A visual project that the teacher could look over and compare to a rubric might be quicker to grade than a stack of tests.

"Are you enjoying your stay?"

She eyed the wine in her glass. Wine didn't belong in a box or can. It belonged in a bottle. Now that she had some, though, she had no other choice but to drink it. "It's been very relaxing." She sipped her drink, expecting it to be the worst thing she'd ever tasted. "Mmm, that's good." The words left her lips before she could stop them.

Candace nodded as she moved toward the oven. "When a friend of mine told me she loved this brand, I was skeptical because wine in a box didn't seem right. But now it's one of my favorites."

From down the hall, she heard a door open and then close. Soon after, Tiegan and Mrs. Wright entered the room. Neither wore any shoes, and water dripped down their faces.

Should she have taken her shoes off when she came in? She never removed them at home, and it honestly hadn't occurred to her to do so now. She glanced over at Candace's feet. Unlike her daughter, the woman had on sneakers. Maybe the recent arrivals had removed theirs because, much like their hair, they'd gotten wet on the walk over.

"Nana and I finished my project. The paint just needs to dry." Tiegan headed straight for the refrigerator and pulled out a gallon of milk.

Candace cleared her throat and looked in her daughter's direction. "Aren't you forgetting something?"

The young girl paused with one hand on a glass in the cabinet and smiled in Juliette's direction. "Hi." She then removed the glass and filled it with milk. "I'm hungry. Is supper almost done?"

"As soon as your uncle gets here, we can eat."

Tiegan didn't need to hear anything else. "I'll go tell him it's time to eat."

"I'm glad you're joining us tonight," Mrs. Wright said as she poured half a glass of wine. "Are you having any issues down at the cottage?"

The heating system could be more efficient, but that didn't qualify as an issue. "No, everything's been great, Mrs. Wright."

The older woman patted Juliette's arm. "We're all adults. Please call me Maggie." She accepted the bowl of roasted potatoes her daughter held out. After setting them on the table, she removed a large garden salad from the refrigerator. "Do you need anything? I'm heading to the grocery store tomorrow anyway."

Tiegan's voice traveled into the room, announcing her arrival. Juliette resisted the urge to turn around. Perhaps over the past twenty-four hours, her mind had embellished her memory of him. Maybe she'd turn around and find he was about as good looking as Mr. Yates, her chemistry teacher junior year. While the man knew the subject well, he hadn't been blessed in the looks department. In fact, he'd always reminded her of a troll from some fairy tale.

Rather than turn and stare—she despised when people did that to her—she reached for her wineglass. "Nope. Mrs. Lambert made sure I had enough to supply a small army."

Unlike his niece, who'd entered the room without even a glance in her direction earlier, Aaron stopped next to the counter. "It's nice to see you again."

She wouldn't call his tone friendly, but rather polite. The type you might use when you're seventeen and your parents are introducing you to one of their business acquaintances, but all you want to do is escape out the door so that you can spend time with friends. And she would know. She'd used the same tone more times than she remembered.

"Hi, Mom." He gave Maggie a quick hug before pouring himself a glass of wine. "Can I do anything, Candace?" Turning, Aaron leaned against the counter.

Nope, her mind had not done any embellishing. As Holly had said during their conversation, the man was panty-melting hot. And his voice melted any other piece of clothing a woman might be wearing. Later tonight, when the man in question wasn't standing in front of her, she'd reassess her earlier opinion that getting involved with someone up here was a bad idea. Because at the moment, getting better acquainted with the man across from her in a variety of ways seemed like a phenomenal idea.

Aaron's sister collected her wineglass and the platter of meat she'd carved. "Nope. Everything is ready."

THEY'D NEVER FORMALLY DEVELOPED a seating plan, but over the last seven months, they'd all adopted an assigned spot at the table. Tonight wasn't any different, which meant his niece sat on one side of him, his mom sat on the other, and Juliette, their guest of honor, sat across from him. Much of the day, Aaron had expected to hear she'd decided to bail on dinner tonight. Rather than cancel, she'd showed up right on time. And he knew she'd arrived on time because he'd seen her car approaching the house from his office window.

Stabbing a potato, he glanced at his sister. Never in his life had they invited guests at the campground to eat dinner with them. The only explanation he could come up with for why his sister did so was because Juliette was not only a guest but also a friend of Holly's. Whatever the reason behind her invitation, he hoped his sister didn't extend too many more invitations. Switching his gaze, he looked at his mom. When he'd heard her asking if Juliette needed anything, he'd come to a dead stop for a minute. Large resorts and five-star hotels might allow guests to put in grocery orders and have them delivered to their door, but the campground had never provided such a service. And as far as he knew, it wasn't one his mom intended to start. So why was she offering to pick up food for their guest now? Was it because the woman across the table was Holly's friend? His mom and Mrs. Lambert were friends, so maybe she felt obligated to make sure Juliette's stay was enjoyable. Or she was asking because Juliette Belmont came from one of the wealthiest families in the United States, and she felt compelled to bend over backward for her? His mom never struck him as a person who would care about a person's background. Perhaps he'd been wrong. Whatever the case, he hoped his mom didn't make a habit of doing their guest's shopping. She had enough of her own responsibilities. She didn't need to be taking on someone else's, especially when the individual was an adult capable of taking care of herself.

"When is there going to be another dance class?" Tiegan asked after she finished filling them all in on her day—a day that, according to her, had been the worst one ever because she had to work with Jeremy Benson on a group project. Aaron didn't know if she'd always disliked the other student, but at least since she'd been living with him, Jeremy was her least favorite kid in her class.

Candace added another slice of meat to her plate and shrugged. "I'm not sure. Hopefully soon. I left a message with the parks and rec office. They haven't called me back yet."

Frowning, Tiegan slumped in her chair and poked at her salad with her fork. "Can't you try again? Kellie and I really want to dance."

"If I don't hear from them by Friday, I'll call again." His sister tapped Tiegan on the shoulder. "Please sit up."

"Isn't there a dance school in town?" Juliette asked.

"No," Tiegan answered. Although she no longer slouched, her pout remained fixed on her face as she pushed aside a radish before taking a forkful of salad.

Tonight wasn't the first time this topic came up over dinner. And until Candace was teaching another dance class at one of the schools' gyms, it would come up again. Each time, his niece's reaction would be similar, not that he blamed her. At her age, he would've been disappointed too if he hadn't been able to participate in the sports he loved.

"There used to be. But Merry and her husband decided to move to Arizona after he retired, so the school closed last year after the recital in June. Two of us that worked there now teach dance classes through the parks and rec department. But we have to compete for space with the other programs offered, so it's not something we can do year-round," Candace explained.

"That's unfortunate. There aren't any dance schools nearby, either?"

His mom shook her head as she buttered a roll. "The closest one is a little over an hour away. A few kids in town go there, but not many. It's just too inconvenient."

"My friend Jasmine goes to Premier Dance. She showed everyone a picture of her recital costumes today," Tiegan added, referring to her friend and classmate Jasmine Pine.

Not that Tiegan knew it, but when his sister and niece moved in, he'd offered to drive her to and from dance once a week because he knew his sister didn't have the time. She'd refused to take him up on the offer. Her rationale had been that classes were already underway, and Tiegan would be behind everyone else. He had a feeling that wasn't her only reason for not accepting his help.

"I danced for a long time. I even minored in it when I was in college. My favorite was ballet. What's yours?" Juliette asked.

Yep, he could picture her up on stage performing a graceful ballet routine with those incredibly long legs of hers. Unlike the first time they met, today she wore dark gray leggings instead of jeans. He'd thought her jeans had shown off her legs well. He'd been dead wrong. It should be illegal for the woman across from him to wear leggings out in public. She'd paired them with a long white sweater that reached almost midthigh. He couldn't decide if that was a good thing or not, since it covered what he suspected was an incredible ass. But if it hadn't been covered, he would've stood there and stared when she walked over to the table earlier. And knowing his luck, Candace would've noticed his behavior. She always picked up on those things he'd rather she missed.

"Tap and hip-hop. But Mom only teaches ballet and jazz. And Miss Sandy teaches lyrical." Tiegan raised her fork toward her mouth, but it didn't make it there. "Oh, and I really like acro too. I took that with Miss Sandy before Dance Dynamics closed."

"I never did acro, but I used to enjoy tap."

He'd always dreaded the tap numbers when his parents dragged him to his sisters' yearly recitals. It wasn't so much the style of the dance but the noise. How anyone survived being in a class with ten or twelve students all tap dancing away was one of the world's great mysteries.

"Since we use the gyms in the schools, we're limited to what we can teach. The tap shoes would ruin the floors, and we don't have the necessary mats for acro classes."

He'd never thought much about it, but his sister's explanation made sense.

Next to him, Tiegan stuffed the last forkful of food in her

mouth and pushed back her chair as she chewed. "I'm done. Can I go?"

"Make sure you take care of your dish first."

His niece didn't need to hear anything else from her mom. After scraping the last few pieces of lettuce and the radishes she didn't eat into the trash, she popped the dish in the dishwasher and bolted from the room.

Across from him, Juliette finished her salad. He'd noticed that while she added some roast and potatoes to her plate, she filled the bulk of the space with salad, which she'd proceeded to eat minus the dressing, unlike his sister, who drowned hers in creamy ranch as usual.

"It's too bad someone who worked at the studio couldn't take it over when the owner retired," Juliette commented.

If his sister had been in a position to own a business, he believed she would've taken over Dance Dynamics in a heartbeat.

For the next few minutes, Juliette and his sister discussed their favorite memories of dancing and why they believed it was such a beneficial activity for girls as well as boys. Candace retrieved dessert from the refrigerator somewhere during their debate of which was a more enjoyable style to perform, contemporary or lyrical. Contemporary got his sister's vote, while Juliette's went toward lyrical.

Juliette accepted the slice of cheesecake covered with cherries from his sister. Perhaps once a week, they had dessert with dinner. Sometimes it would be something either his sister or mom baked. Other nights it'd just be a bowl of ice cream. When they did have dessert though, it was usually on the weekend or for a special occasion, not a random Tuesday night. But he wouldn't complain. Cheesecake, regardless of whether it was New York-style topped with fruit or the one his mom made using ricotta cheese, was his all-time favorite dessert.

"This might seem like an odd question, and I didn't want to mention it in front of Tiegan, but have you ever considered letting her do some modeling?"

Aaron choked on the water he'd unfortunately just swallowed. He'd never deny his niece was beautiful. When she got to high school, she'd have guys lining up at her door. Already he was dreading when the time came because he'd been a high school boy. He knew how most of them thought. Tiegan's beauty aside, he didn't want to see her get involved in the modeling world. From the little he'd seen in the media, it wasn't a kid-friendly lifestyle, and Tiegan might not want to admit it, and she might sometimes act older than her age, but she was still a child.

Candace passed him a slice of cake before cutting one for herself. "Not seriously, no. But I've always thought she was beautiful enough to do some modeling. I'm not even sure she'd be interested."

"If she is and you're okay with it, I can get you in touch with my agent, Pierre. I've been with him since I started out. He's got his quirks, but he's a great guy to work with and knows the business better than anyone I've ever met."

Aaron stuffed a large forkful of cheesecake in his mouth to avoid telling their guest what he really thought of her idea. As he chewed, he looked over at his sister. He recognized the expression on Candace's face. He'd seen it enough times over the years to know she was considering Juliette's suggestion.

"Let me think about it and talk to her. Honestly, I have no idea if she'd be interested or not. And I'll let you know."

"No pressure. Whatever you decide is fine. I just think she could have a phenomenal career. And Pierre is great. I think you'd like him."

Like a magnet, her voice pulled his gaze in her direction. Much to his annoyance, he couldn't look away as her lips closed around a forkful of dessert. The image of him removing the fork and replacing it with his lips formed.

He didn't daydream, so he didn't know why his mind was conjuring up images now. Maybe it had something to do with the fact that Juliette's lips, like everything else about her, were perfect. Or at least perfect in his eyes. They were full, but they looked natural, not as if a doctor had injected them with chemicals.

"Mmm. This is delicious. Did you make it?" she asked, cutting another forkful off her piece. "I wish I could bake like this."

"Come over one night I don't have class, and I'll show you. Making cheesecake isn't hard."

Yep, he'd expected his sister's offer as soon as Juliette asked if Candace baked the cake. She'd always been a social butterfly willing to help or teach someone else.

"Sounds good."

For the second time that day, Juliette surprised Aaron by finishing her entire slice. While Candace walked her to the door, he cleaned up the few dishes left on the table. Overall, the evening hadn't been as unpleasant as he'd feared. That didn't mean he wanted to do it again anytime soon. He didn't consider himself shy in the least, but he preferred to spend his time with friends and loved ones, especially when he was in his own home. At the moment, he didn't know Juliette well enough to determine if he liked her or not. And since she wouldn't be around long, he saw no reason to waste his time learning.

"Thanks for taking care of those." Candace entered the kitchen and retrieved her iced tea from the table.

Before he launched into the discussion he wanted, Aaron closed the dishwasher and turned it on. Then he leaned back against the counter and picked up his drink. "You're not seriously going to consider Juliette's offer, are you?"

"About letting Tiegan model?"

No, the one about her giving you a million dollars. "Yeah."

His sister nodded. "I'm not sold one way or the other on the idea. And I'd need to talk to her first. She might not be interested, and I'd never force her." She took a sip of tea before she continued. "Who knows, it might be a way for her to help pay for college down the road."

Even if it helped his niece afford college at some point, he didn't want her trying it. "I think you should forget Juliette ever mentioned it, Candace. It's more important she focus on school and having fun with her friends."

"Who says she can't do all three?"

"I don't see it happening." The guest in Cottage 10 was the first celebrity he'd had dinner with, but he'd seen enough internet stories and magazine covers to know children thrust into the spotlight had anything but a normal life. And more often than not, they struggled as adults because of it.

"First of all, I never said I intended to speak with Juliette's agent. And second, Tiegan might not even be interested. So, relax." She patted him on the shoulder as she walked by on her way out of the room.

Relax? Right. When Mom had first told him who their long-term guest was, he'd worried she'd be trouble. Looked like he might have been right.

CHAPTER 6

"IT SMELLS GOOD." Juliette eyed the lemon-blueberry upside down cake Candace, her new friend and baking teacher, set down on the counter. It was the third dessert she'd made with the other woman's help.

As promised, Candace had shown her how to make a New York-style cheesecake the Friday after she first joined them for dinner. It'd been far easier than she'd anticipated. In fact, Juliette believed she'd have no problem making it again on her own. A few days later, she'd attempted double chocolate chip brownies. That time she'd received instruction more or less from Tiegan rather than Candace. But either way, they'd come out fantastic, and she'd eaten far more than she should have.

Candace pulled a knife from the drawer and handed it to her. Then she pulled two plates from the cupboard. "Cut it and let's see."

She cut one sliver and put it on a plate.

"You can have that one. Make mine a little bigger," Candace said before Juliette cut a second helping.

After cutting a slice about twice as wide as hers, Juliette

dug into her piece. The combination of sweet blueberries and tart lemon exploded on her tongue, and immediately she wished she'd given herself a larger portion. "Man, this is good. If I didn't make it, I'd think it came from a bakery." She washed it down with some tea before she got another forkful. "When Curt and his fiancée come to visit, I might have to make this for them. Or maybe the cheesecake. That was great too. He'll never believe I made it."

"Is that the same cousin who visited you last week?"

Juliette nodded as she popped the last of her cake in her mouth and cut another equally small sliver. "He's only about two hours away. Curt and Taylor will probably bring Reese with them when they come. She's Taylor's niece. I think she'd get along well with Tiegan. She's... I'm not sure how old she is, but she's around Tiegan's age."

Come to think of it, she didn't know how old Tiegan was either. If she had to guess, she'd say eleven or twelve, but it was possible the girl was simply tall for her age. "How old is Tiegan anyway?"

"She'll be eleven next month." Candace took another bite of cake before she spoke again. "Does Reese live with her aunt?"

"She lives with Taylor and her grandmother next door to my cousin. That's how Curt and Taylor met. But when they get married, Taylor and Reese will move in with Curt. As far as I know, Taylor has been Reese's guardian since she was a baby. Reese's mom, Taylor's sister, is not exactly mother material." She saw no reason to go into the unpleasant details.

Candace gave a little sarcastic laugh and reached for the knife. "Yeah, some people should not become parents." She cut a not-so-little second slice of cake and added it to her plate. "My ex-husband is one of them. Tiegan hasn't seen Eric in almost a year. And I don't think she's talked to him since Christmas."

Growing up, Juliette had seen her father more or less every day except when he traveled for business, or she'd attended boarding school. And when she had been away at school, she'd talked to both her parents on a weekly basis. Even now, she saw them frequently and spoke with them often.

"That's too bad. Does he live nearby?" Not that it would excuse his behavior, but if he'd moved to the west coast or something because of work, it would make regular visits difficult.

The other woman stabbed her cake with a little more force than necessary. "Who knows? The handful of times he's sent child support, the postmark on the envelope is from a different place. He bought an RV right before he left Avon, and he's been traveling around the country with his new girlfriend. Even before the divorce, Eric worked remotely, so I'm sure that's what he's still doing. And I don't know much about his girlfriend, but I know she's—" Candace stopped abruptly and cleared her throat. "She doesn't need to work."

Her new friend sounded a little bitter, and Juliette didn't blame her one bit. It was bad enough her ex-husband didn't play an active role in his daughter's life. But the least the creep could do was send child support payments.

"It's part of the reason why Tiegan and I are living here with Aaron."

She'd wondered why they called Aaron's house home but hadn't wanted to pry. She hated it when people poked their noses into her life. She saw no reason Candace would feel any differently about it.

"Before the divorce, what I made substituting at the schools and teaching dance was enough, since Eric worked full-time."

During a previous conversation, she'd learned Candace worked almost every day as a substitute in the town. While she preferred to work in the elementary school, she worked in whatever building the district needed her.

"Even if Dance Dynamics hadn't closed, what I brought home wasn't enough to pay the rent on the apartment we lived in and cover all the other expenses. I thought about quitting school again, so I could get a second job at night waitressing or something." She paused and sipped her tea. "Let's just say Aaron didn't like the idea. He's always been an overprotective big brother. He suggested we move in with him at least until I finish my bachelor's degree."

Candace had mentioned before she was taking night classes, but Juliette didn't know what she was studying or where.

"At first, it was a little odd not only living with my brother but also in the house I grew up in. But it works out pretty well for everyone. Since Aaron works mostly from home and Mom's right next door, when I go to class, there's always someone around for Tiegan to stay with. My brother refuses to let me pay rent, so I pay the electric bill, and I do most of the cooking and cleaning." Stepping back, she opened the refrigerator and removed the pitcher of iced tea.

Not only was the man handsome, but by the sound of it, he valued family. She couldn't say the same about most of the men she'd been attracted to, including Daniel. No question about it: she was attracted to Aaron.

Every time she saw him, and she'd seen him several times now, she had to remind herself she wasn't here to get romantically involved. And each time it took a little more convincing, because literally all the man had to do was walk in the room and her pulse rate went up a few notches— something she had to admit was a unique experience. Usually, it took a hell of a lot more to get her excited. Heaven help her if Aaron ever did any of those things to her.

"Got to love overprotective brothers." She adored Scott and couldn't ask for a better brother, but he had his moments.

"Is yours older or younger?"

She'd assumed Candace knew all about her family. The people she normally associated with always knew precisely who lingered on the many branches of her family tree. "Older. I also have several male cousins who act almost as bad. I also have an older sister."

Candace nodded as she refilled first Juliette's cup and then her own. "She married J.T. Williamson. I saw the pictures on the cover of *Today Magazine* last month. Your brother got married last year, didn't he?"

Scott's wedding hadn't attracted quite as many headlines as Courtney's wedding, but it certainly hadn't gone unnoticed. "Yep. And he and his wife are expecting twins in June."

"Speaking of brothers, Aaron is single."

Juliette racked her brain for an adequate response to the out-of-the-blue statement. Before she thought of one, Candace spoke again.

"And I don't think he's been on a date since I've been living here." She put the pitcher back in the fridge before she returned to the barstool near the counter. "And yes, I've seen the way you look at him when he's not paying attention."

She thought she'd done a better job of not staring during dinner. If she joined them again for a meal, she needed to be more careful.

"I know I'm a little biased, but Aaron's a great guy. I think you should ask him out for coffee or something."

Juliette blew out a breath and considered her response. "Believe me, I've thought about it. I'm not sure getting involved with anyone right now is a good idea." She waited for Candace's attempt to change her mind. It was something Holly or several of her other friends would do in this situation.

73

"Fair enough. I won't bring it up again, but think about it."

Oh, Aaron would pop into her thoughts whether Candace mentioned him again or not. Whether she'd change her mind about asking him out, though, was anyone's guess. "Did you hear back from the parks and rec office?"

The last time she'd joined the family for dinner, Candace mentioned she'd left another message with the director there.

Nodding, Candace sighed. "Yesterday. The high school and middle school gyms are booked until June for a spring basketball league. And the elementary gym is being used for senior yoga and futsal. Sandy and I have the high school gym every Saturday for three hours in June and July. My daughter wasn't happy when I told her."

When she was Tiegan's age, anything more than a week or two felt like a lifetime away. "That stinks."

It doesn't hurt to ask. The half-baked idea had popped into her head over the weekend and refused to leave. One of the reasons she'd come up here was to make some decisions about her life. She'd always loved dancing. Even now, she sometimes missed it. So maybe the crazy idea bouncing around in her head deserved some serious thought. And the question on the tip of her tongue would factor into any long-term decisions she made.

"Before it closed, did the dance school in town have a lot of students?"

"Probably between two hundred and fifty to three hundred. Not only kids from Avon danced there. We had a decent number of students from Ashford and a few from Danielson. The studio was much smaller when I started dancing there."

The schools she'd trained at had been bigger, but she'd also grown up much closer to Boston. However, two hundred and fifty students would be enough to keep a small dance school in business. "What happened to the space when the owner retired?" A location already set up as a studio would make opening a new one a much quicker and possibly less expensive process.

"It's been for sale since Merry retired. I don't think anyone has looked at it. Why?"

Juliette shrugged slightly and reached for her drink. At the moment, she didn't care to share her crazy notion with anyone. "Just curious."

COMING around the bend in the driveway, Aaron spotted Juliette's car parked out front. The sight of it didn't surprise him. She'd become a frequent visitor over the past week and a half. Sometimes she joined them for dinner, and other times she got baking lessons from his sister. Considering the time of day, either was a possible reason for her current visit.

After parking in the garage, Aaron grabbed his jacket and computer bag from the back seat. He'd had a meeting with Stephen, his department head, at work today, so he'd spent the day working in Boston rather than at home. As much as he enjoyed the convenience of working from home, sometimes it was nice to go into the office. It not only gave him a change of scenery, but it allowed him to see his coworkers somewhere other than on a computer monitor. If it didn't involve dealing with the traffic into and out of the city, he'd do it more often.

The scent of something fresh-baked greeted him when he entered the kitchen. Both his sister and Juliette sat at the counter chatting away. They each had empty plates in front of them, and he hoped they hadn't finished whatever they'd baked.

"Hi," he said, closing the door into the garage.

"You're home earlier than I expected," his sister said after both women greeted him.

When he spent the day working in Boston, it was anyone's guess when he'd get home. Since he'd arrived at the office long before just about everyone else today, he'd left right after his meeting with Stephen to avoid the worst of the traffic.

"Is there any more of what you baked left?" He'd eaten a rather early lunch and nothing since.

Candace pointed toward some kind of cake on the counter near them. "Have you thought about greeting your eyes checked?"

Although there were pieces missing, the majority of the cake remained. Perhaps if his eyes hadn't been so focused on their guest, he would've seen it himself. It didn't seem to matter how many times he saw Juliette, he had trouble looking at anything but her when they were in the same room.

"I'll add it to my to-do list." After leaving his stuff on a kitchen chair, he got a dish from the cupboard. "What is it?" He pointed toward the cake with a knife. He didn't wait for an answer before cutting into it, because, in the end, it didn't really matter. When it came to food, he wasn't fussy, and it smelled great.

"Lemon-blueberry upside down cake," Juliette answered. Her voice pulled all his attention her way. "Today's baking lesson."

He didn't bother with a fork. Instead, he ripped a chunk off the slice he'd cut and popped it in his mouth. "It's delicious."

His compliment earned him an immediate smile from Juliette, and for a moment, he could not look at anything but her.

"I planned to order pizza for dinner tonight. Anything specific you want?"

Candace's voice broke whatever spell their guest's smile put him under. He dropped his gaze toward the cake and ripped off another piece. "Whatever is fine. You know what I like."

"Do you want to stay and eat with us?" His sister pulled out the menu for Bruno's Pizza and opened it.

Juliette shook her head, causing the few pieces of hair that had escaped her braid to sway. "Not tonight, thanks." She tucked the stray pieces behind her ears the way he wanted to. "But if you don't mind, I'll take a piece of cake home with me."

"Take the whole thing if you want."

Please don't. Aaron would want a second slice later. He couldn't get one if the cake was down in cottage number ten.

"No, I just want a piece."

While his sister wrapped up a substantial slice, he grabbed the menu she'd taken out. He hadn't lied. He didn't care what kind of pizza she ordered, but looking at the menu gave his eyes something to do other than stare at their guest. The traitorous things had a mind of their own whenever Juliette was in the same room.

"Are you sure there isn't something specific you want?" Candace asked once they were alone.

Well, maybe, but it wasn't available from Bruno's Pizza. He pushed the menu across the counter toward her. "Whatever you want."

Her eyebrow inched ever so slightly up, but she didn't say anything. Instead, she called in an order before retaking her seat. Before she could spew out whatever was on her mind, and he knew something was tumbling around in her head, he needed to start a conversation.

Following his and Tiegan's conversation at George's Diner, he'd run the idea of getting his niece tickets to the ballet by his sister, since she was the one who would have to take her. Although she'd argued it was potentially an expensive gift, she'd given him the green light. He'd hoped for something much later in the spring or perhaps the early summer, since Tiegan's birthday wasn't until April, and although the calendar claimed spring had arrived, it didn't mean they couldn't still get some nasty wintery weather. Last year, they'd gotten eight inches of snow on April Fool's Day. If a late season storm hit, he'd prefer his sister or mother didn't find themselves stuck driving in it.

"I got tickets for Tiegan to see *Swan Lake* on Saturday night with you and Mom for her birthday. And I booked a hotel room for the three of you to stay in the city for three nights since Tiegan doesn't have school on Monday. The show is leaving Boston at the end of March, and there isn't another ballet being performed in the city until November." In his mind, making an eleven-year-old wait more than seven months to see a show wasn't an option.

"One night would've been sufficient."

Aaron knew that. But this was Tiegan's first birthday since Eric walked out on her and Candace. He wanted to make it as special as possible. "The hotel has a pool. Good luck getting Tiegan out of it."

"Since you'll have the house all to yourself for the weekend, maybe you should have a little fun."

Her tone told him the kind of fun she had in mind. And while he hadn't been on a date or had any woman over since his sister and niece moved in, it wasn't only because they were there. Aaron hadn't met anyone he wanted to spend time with.

"Did the town get an influx of women between the ages of twenty-five and forty-five? Because if not, there isn't anyone in Avon I'd want to spend my weekend with."

Candace steepled her fingers underneath her chin. "Liar."

Like every other human on Earth, he'd told the occasional

little white lie from time to time. Now wasn't one of those times. "If you think I'm interested in Nelly, you're wrong. Besides, isn't she with Jeff?" The previous summer, he and Nelly had gone out a few times, but it never developed into anything. Now, if they saw each other at the store or George's, they said hello and went about their business.

"Wow, you're being difficult. I'm talking about our guest in Cottage 10. You can't take your eyes off her whenever she's here."

She'd already called him a liar anyway, so he might as well prove her right. "You're imagining things."

"*Please.* We both know I'm not. While we're gone, invite Juliette up for dinner. Who knows what will happen."

Any additional denials wouldn't help him, but the truth might. "If she was Juliette Belmont, high school English teacher or accountant from New York, I'd consider it." He'd never gotten involved with any of the campground's guests, but then they'd never had a guest stay as long as she planned to, either. "But not heiress Juliette Belmont. We both know people like her live in a world that plays by a different set of rules."

"That just might be the dumbest thing you've ever said. And you've said some stupid stuff in the past."

"Huh, then if Bryon's parents had been schoolteachers instead of multimillionaires, he still would've gotten only three years of probation, right?"

Candace scowled and crossed her arms over her chest. "You're right. Stuff like that unfortunately happens. But I still like Juliette, and if you asked her up for dinner or to a movie, I'm confident she would say yes."

At least every time he'd been around her, she'd been nice enough. She never put on airs or talked down to anyone in the family. And much to her credit, she hadn't tried to change anyone's mind when Candace told her Tiegan wasn't interested in modeling. That didn't mean he wanted to get involved with her.

"And I didn't say you couldn't be friends with her and spend time together. I just do not want to." Standing, he retrieved his jacket and computer bag from the kitchen chair. "I'll be right back."

Aaron dropped off his laptop in his office before continuing upstairs to his bedroom so he could put away his jacket, which he usually hung in the closet near the front door. Today though, he wanted a few minutes alone to deal with the emotions his conversation with Candace brought up.

Born nine months apart, he and Troy had been more like brothers than cousins. They'd played on the same sports team, hung out with the same friends, and graduated high school together. Hell, they'd even taken a set of identical twins to their senior prom. Even when they'd gone off to college, they'd seen each other all the time, since they'd both attended in-state universities. And seven years ago when his mom called and told him Troy had been killed in a car accident, it'd been like losing a cousin, best friend, and brother all at once. An accident caused by a Bryon Casella, a seventeen-year-old who'd been as high as a kite and behind the wheel of his wealthy parents' SUV. While both cars had been totaled, Casella and his sister had walked away without a scratch on them while Troy died before the EMTs even reached the crash site, and his girlfriend spent weeks in the hospital. As if that wasn't bad enough, Casella's high-priced lawyers from Boston saved him from serving any jail time. Instead, the judge suspended his license for two years and gave him probation, proving to Aaron that a different set of rules applied to the wealthy. And at least in the United States, there weren't too many people wealthier than their long-term guest —a woman he would be polite to whenever he was around her, but not one he intended to get to know any better.

The sound of the doorbell disturbed the silence in the room. A moment or two later, he heard feet running down the hallway.

Grabbing the ballet tickets from his jacket pocket, Aaron stuffed his thoughts of Troy back into the corner of his mind where they usually resided and left the room.

CHAPTER 7

SATURDAY MORNING, Aaron rolled onto his back and opened his eyes. As if Clifford had been sitting there just waiting for some sign Aaron was awake, the dog jumped on the bed. Yesterday, Candace, Tiegan, and his mom left for Boston as soon as his niece stepped off the bus. With his usual bed partner gone, Clifford slept on the dog bed in Aaron's room, the spot he'd always used at bedtime before Tiegan moved in and invited the dog to sleep with her.

At first, he'd been against letting Clifford sleep in Tiegan's bed because at some point Tiegan wouldn't be living there, and he didn't want the dog to suddenly be jumping into his bed at night. When he suggested they put the dog bed in her room instead, she went along with it, although there had been a lot of pouting involved. At least, they had thought she'd gone along with it. But then Candace started finding the dog in his niece's bed almost every morning when she went to wake Tiegan up for school. After that short-lived experiment, Aaron put the dog bed back in his room, and Clifford slept with his niece, which meant last night was the first time the dog had used it in months. He hadn't been happy about it either. Twice, the dog had jumped on the bed, and Aaron had to move him back to the floor.

"Hey, bud." He scratched the dog behind the ear and reached for his watch on the nightstand. The combination of room-darkening shades and curtains blocked out a significant amount of sunlight, making it difficult to gauge the time.

Almost six-thirty. No wonder his dog was not only awake but watching the bed for any signs of life. He wanted to eat. Tiegan got up early for school, and she fed the dog as soon as she came downstairs. He'd never assigned the chore to her; she'd simply taken it upon herself when she moved in.

"You want to eat." At the word "eat," the dog's tail wagged. Aaron raked his hands down his face and then stared at the ceiling.

If it was up to him, he'd stay in bed for another hour or two. With the house to himself for the first time in seven months, he'd stayed up late watching movies he enjoyed. Movies that had a lot of action and often a lot of swearing. The type his niece was too young to watch, and his sister hated. Or he'd done that until the power went out around midnight.

The icy rain and hail accompanied by strong winds had started sometime around nine. Earlier in the day, the meteorologist had predicted the storm would begin around dinner-time, which was one of the reasons his sister insisted they leave when they did. He hadn't been surprised when the storm didn't begin on time. After all, this was New England. And if New England weather was anything, it was unpredictable. It also hadn't shocked him when the power went out, considering the wind gusts outside. Later, when he got around to going outside, he'd no doubt find some downed limbs on the property.

What he wanted right now made little difference. Until he

got up and fed Clifford, the dog wouldn't leave him alone, which would make falling back to sleep impossible.

Chilly air greeted him when he tossed back the blankets, and he didn't need to try the lamp next to his bed to know the power was still out. After pulling on the flannel pajama bottoms he'd tossed at the end of the bed, he pulled on a sweatshirt and some wool socks. As if he knew exactly what Aaron intended, Clifford jumped off the bed and waited by the bedroom door.

"I'm coming. I'm coming." In response, the dog wagged his tail again, and as soon as Aaron opened the door, he bolted into the hallway. When he reached the stairs, he turned and looked back to make sure Aaron followed.

Growing up, they'd always had a small generator to power the water pump on the well, because without water, it was impossible to flush the toilet or wash your hands. After purchasing the home from his mom, he'd replaced it with a slightly larger one that could also power the refrigerator. More than once when he was a kid, they'd lost power, and as a result, all the food in the fridge. He'd considered getting something powerful enough to run the heating system and all the electrical outlets in the home too. In the end, he'd decided the cost wasn't worth it. The house had a woodstove that did a decent job of heating the first floor, and he made sure he was never without wood no matter the time of year. Plus, when they lost power, it usually wasn't for very long. Only once could he remember losing it for more than two days. He'd been twelve, and an early winter storm consisting of heavy wet snow brought down tree limbs and electrical wires across the state. The entire town had been without power for five days. While they'd had at least heat thanks to the woodstove and running water, many of their neighbors hadn't been so lucky. In fact, his cousin Troy, his sister, and their parents had stayed with them until the electric company restored the power.

Like he often did when he reached the bottom of the stairs, he flipped up the light switch. "Idiot, the power is out," he muttered.

Rather than continue to the kitchen, his usual first stop when he came downstairs in the morning, Aaron kneeled next to the woodstove and grabbed some firewood from the log rack as well as some kindling. Not surprisingly, Clifford, who'd already made it halfway to the kitchen, turned around when he realized Aaron no longer followed him and headed back in his direction. After parking his butt next to him, the dog started whining while Aaron worked on getting a fire going in the woodstove.

"I get it. You want to eat." And he wanted some heat. "You've got a fur coat on. I don't." He paused long enough to pet the dog before retrieving the matches he kept in a drawer.

Confident the fire wouldn't go out, he closed the load door and stood. "Okay, Clifford, let's fill that belly of yours." He'd rather avoid any additional complaints from his four-legged friend this morning.

Once he had the dog momentarily satisfied—he would undoubtedly beg for some of Aaron's breakfast once he sat down—Aaron got the teakettle from the cupboard. He preferred coffee to hot tea, but since he couldn't make any, he'd settle for caffeine in whatever form he could get it. And unless he wanted a can of cola, tea was all he had available.

For years, his parents had used an electric stove in the kitchen. When he'd had the room remodeled, he'd replaced it with a gas one instead. Not only did he prefer it for cooking, an activity he'd done almost every night until Candace moved in, but at times like this, it allowed him or whoever else was here to prepare a hot meal or boil water. And while he waited for the stove to do just that, he got the box of oatmeal from the pantry. Since he was boiling water anyway, a bowl of oatmeal would be a quick, easy, and, more importantly, warm breakfast. Precisely what this morning called for.

JULIETTE'S PHONE ringing penetrated her sleep and brought her pleasant dream to an abrupt and unsatisfying end. Rolling onto her side, she looked at the offending device on the nightstand. The name Daniel Green greeted her.

Seriously. Her dream had been ruined by that creep. She didn't bother to answer. There wasn't a single thing he could say to excuse his behavior. Later, when she moved from the comfort of her bed, she'd delete his number from her contact list. Why she hadn't already done so was a mystery to her.

She moved onto her back again and stared up at the ceiling. Was the power still out? Around one o'clock or so, she'd woken up to use the bathroom only to discover the storm had knocked out the electricity. When the power went out at her condo, she didn't think twice about it, since the building had emergency generators to ensure that the heat and the elevators worked. It was a similar case at her parents' home, although there the generator kept every appliance and light working, making power outages no big deal.

The cottage didn't have any backup systems. While it didn't matter to her if she could turn on a light, especially at the moment, she cared about the heat. Although the outside temperature was most likely higher than if it'd still been January, no one would consider it toasty.

Reaching over, she tried the lamp on the nightstand. "Great," she muttered when it didn't switch on. She shoved her arm back under the blankets. In the city, service crews usually got things up and running again fairly quickly. But what about here? According to her phone, it was already nine o'clock. That meant the power had been out for at least eight hours. Perhaps even much longer, since last night she'd been unusually tired and had gone to bed before ten, an almost unheard-of event when she was in the city. Heck, some nights, she was just going out around that time.

With no place to be and nothing waiting for her except the new novel she'd started yesterday, she stayed under the covers until an empty stomach forced her to leave the comfort and relative warmth of her bed. Even before she made it down to the kitchen, she was reconsidering her decision. The unpleasant rumble she felt in her stomach as she weighed how much longer she could go without eating sent her across the living room rather than back up to her bedroom.

In the kitchen, she pulled out the eggs and dropped two slices of bread in the toaster before removing a pan from the cabinet. After cracking the eggs into it, she carried the pan over to the stove and came to a dead stop.

"Dumb, dumb." She shook her head. Unlike at home, the cottage had an electric stove, so unless she managed to start a fire in the middle of the kitchen, she wouldn't be cooking eggs or anything else this morning. But hey, it wasn't like she'd starve or anything. She still had bread and plenty of peanut butter. She'd make herself a sandwich and keep her fingers crossed that by lunchtime, the stove and every other appliance in the cottage worked again.

Removing the bread from the toaster, she opened both the peanut butter and marshmallow fluff Mrs. Lambert purchased for her weeks ago but that she'd yet to touch. Thoughts of wrapping herself in a few more layers kept her from eating slowly and lingering in the kitchen. According to the thermostat on the wall, the inside temperature had dropped to fifty-nine already. Fifty-nine degrees might be fine for a nice brisk walk outside while bundled up, but when it referred to the temperature of her living room, it was another story.

I'm not going to freeze to death. She had several sweat-shirts and blankets. She'd just head upstairs, add on another layer, and wrap herself in a blanket. And if she got really desperate, she could always go turn on her car and sit inside for a little while to warm up. Yep, having no heat or electricity wasn't the end of the world. It was merely an inconvenience to deal with today.

Three hours later, she wished Holly had known someone with a cottage on a sparsely populated tropical island instead of a campground in northern New Hampshire. Either that, or that she'd been smart enough to get firewood delivered for the woodstove. Even with multiple layers of clothes on and wrapped in the comforter from her bed, she was cold. And the temperature wasn't the worst of her problems either.

She hadn't considered the source of the cottage's water supply. Never in her life had she needed to. But if she had, she would've known not to flush the toilet and fill her water bottle, because now the well was empty, and without electricity, the pump couldn't refill it, and that meant no water until the power came back.

If some parts of town had electricity, perhaps the Lamberts had heat and running water. Even if they didn't, maybe they had a generator or a fireplace with a raging fire in it. The last time Holly's mom stopped over, she'd once again reminded her to call if she needed anything. You could consider heat something, and she needed it right now. Juliette exchanged her e-reader for her cell phone.

Instead of hearing Mrs. Lambert's voice, Juliette got the woman's voice mail after a few rings. Without leaving a message, she disconnected the call. Unfortunately, Holly had left town on Monday and returned to New York, so there was no point in trying her. That reduced the number of people Juliette knew in town even further, and three of them were in Boston for the weekend. Since the home was on the same property, it wouldn't have power either, but it had a wood-stove. More importantly, she'd seen the log rack full of fire-wood next to it. She didn't doubt that everyone up there, except for perhaps Tiegan, knew how to get a fire going safely.

She didn't have Aaron's phone number, but she could call the office line. If he didn't answer, she could drive up to the house. But then what? While he was polite whenever she saw him, they weren't exactly what you would call friends. Asking a friend to let you hang out and warm up was one thing. Asking a relative stranger if you could come inside until your place had heat again was entirely different.

Before she decided either way, someone knocked on the front door. As if her thoughts had conjured him up, she found Aaron standing on the little porch when she peeked out the window.

"Come on in." As she moved away from the door, she pulled the comforter more tightly around her.

Stepping inside, he closed the door before any more chilly air could make its way inside, as if it really mattered all that much at this point. "I wanted to see how you were doing."

"A little cold." Would he consider it rude if she asked to spend some time at his house? At this point, did she care what he thought of her if it meant her fingers were no longer numb?

His eyes darted toward the woodstove and the empty log rack before he focused on her face again. "You're welcome to come to my house. I don't have power either, but it's warm there."

If it didn't require unwrapping herself from the blankets, she'd hug the man.

"I talked to Robby, a buddy of mine who works for the electric company. Much of the state is out, so it will probably be a while before the power is back. You're welcome to

89

spend the night if it doesn't come back today. I can wait for you to pack a few things, or you can drive up to the house when you're ready."

If she took her car, she wouldn't need him to drive her back once the electricity returned. "I'll meet you up there."

"Sounds good. I'll see you in a few minutes. I'll leave the front door unlocked. Just come in when you get there."

She'd rather not have to stay the night. If the power didn't come back, though, she didn't want to sleep here with no heat or water either, so she tossed a few things, including her toothbrush and e-reader, into one of the reusable shopping bags Mrs. Lambert had left behind and headed out.

The scent of wood burning and Clifford greeted her when she stepped inside Aaron's house. She'd never owned a pet. It wasn't so much because she didn't like animals but more that she didn't want the responsibility of caring for one. She enjoyed being able to come and go as she pleased without having to worry about boarding a furry friend or finding someone to watch it. That being said, she liked Clifford. The mutt—at least she thought he was a mutt because he didn't resemble any breed she was familiar with—was one of the friendliest dogs she'd ever met. And according to Candace, the dog was also protective of Tiegan.

"Hello," she called out as she ran her hand across the dog's head and down his neck.

"Make yourself at home. I'll be right there." Aaron's voice came from the vicinity of the kitchen.

She didn't need to hear his suggestion twice. Juliette left her bag by the door and headed straight for the woodstove. Stripping off her gloves, she held her hands toward it. *Ah, heat.* She closed her eyes and let the warmth roll over her.

"If you sit on the sofa, Clifford will cuddle up next to you. He's almost as good as an electric blanket."

Opening her eyes, she found Aaron standing there, a mug

in each hand. He'd ditched his jacket and wore a dark green flannel shirt over a black thermal undershirt. The flannel shirt amplified the color of his eyes, while the fitted undershirt showcased his chest and trim waist.

"When I left the cottage, you looked like you could use something hot to drink." He handed her one of the steaming mugs. "I didn't know if you liked anything in your tea, so I left it black. But help yourself to the milk and sugar."

First, the man invited her to his blissfully warm house, and now he made her tea. If it wouldn't either make things incredibly awkward or get her kicked out, she'd kiss him. Who was she kidding? She'd been thinking about kissing him all week. Actually, this morning before the phone had so rudely woken her, she'd been about to do more than kiss him in her dream.

"Thank you." Even though she preferred her tea with a splash of milk, she took a sip before setting the mug down so she could remove her jacket. The hot liquid coursed down her throat, warming her insides much like the way the fire was warming her skin. "I hope this doesn't affect the ballet. When I was here Thursday, it was all Tiegan could talk about."

"I got off the phone with my sister right before you got here. They never lost power in Boston."

The words "lucky them" sat on the tip of her tongue. But before she uttered them, she reconsidered. If not for the storm and the lack of electricity, she wouldn't now have an opportunity to get to know Aaron better, something a part of her had wanted to do since she first saw him in the woods. "That's good. I've never seen anyone quite so excited as your niece when she told me about the tickets you got her for her birthday."

.   .   .

WHEN AARON HAD BEEN in high school, he'd worked at the campground in the summer rather than at Gorman's Shop and Save or the fast-food restaurant in Ashford, the two most popular places for teenagers to get part-time jobs. He'd done whatever his dad or the maintenance personnel his parents employed during the season told him to do. They'd never sent him to check on the welfare of a guest. As far as he knew, it wasn't something his parents or any employee ever did either.

Until today.

Although used in the winter, the cottages weren't as well insulated as his house, so whatever heat had been in the cottage before the power went out would quickly escape. Thanks to its size, the woodstove could heat Juliette's whole cottage, making it comfortable. When Juliette had checked in, Mom would've told her she could get firewood from Valley Landscaping. She told everyone who stayed at the campground regardless of the time of year about the company because a lot of people liked to have campfires and they offered the best prices. He hadn't known if Juliette had bothered to call them. And even if she had, he'd doubted the woman would know how to get a fire going.

At first, he'd told himself Juliette and the conditions she found herself in weren't his problem. She was a grown woman and should be able to take care of herself. His conscience disagreed. And throughout the morning, images of her sitting on the sofa with blue lips shivering kept popping up in his head. By lunchtime, they were no longer popping up from time to time but instead stuck there. Even still, when he got in his truck, he hadn't planned on inviting her to stay with him. Instead, he intended to check on her and give her the firewood he'd thrown in the bed of his truck as well as a quick lesson on how to use the woodstove before returning to the comfort of his house.

His nice, quiet, empty house.

When she'd opened the door with the comforter wrapped around her, shivering, his original intention went out the window. At that moment, he'd wanted to wrap his arms around her, pull her in close, and give her whatever body heat he possessed. Before his body could do something completely inappropriate, his mouth invited her to stay with him rather than offer her the wood in the car. With her sitting mere feet away, all he could do was make the best of it and hope he didn't do something stupid like kiss the very lips that had pleasured him last night in his erotic dreams.

"Are you hungry?" Without being able to use the stove or the microwave, she would've been limited as to what she could prepare. "I already ate lunch, but I can make you something." If she wanted food, he could remove himself from the temptation that was Juliette Belmont and not appear rude.

She lowered the mug from her mouth and licked a drop of tea off her bottom lip. Although a perfectly innocent action, his body responded. Yep, he needed to make more of an effort when it came to his social life. Something as simple as a woman licking her bottom lip should not be affecting him unless maybe she sat there naked while doing it.

"No, thanks. I had a peanut butter and fluff sandwich not long before you came."

So much for having an excuse to leave the room. "My mom used to pack me those for lunch a lot when I was a kid." They needed to talk about something. It was either that or sit there and stare at each other.

"Until I was about nine or ten, the only kind of sandwiches I would eat were peanut butter and jelly or peanut butter and fluff."

Food was a nice safe topic. "At least you'd eat a sandwich. My older sister, Elise, wouldn't touch them. It used to drive my mom crazy. When Elise started middle school, Mom gave up and made her get her own lunch ready."

"When I was in middle school, I decided to become a vegetarian. No matter what Paulette prepared for dinner, if it contained meat, I wouldn't touch it. My brother and sister thought I'd lost my mind. I lasted three months before the need for a hamburger did me in."

He didn't know who Paulette was, and he didn't intend to ask. However, based on the little he knew about Juliette, he assumed she was an employee of her parents. "Yeah, I wouldn't even make it three weeks without meat. Salads are great as an add-on, but they're not a main meal."

SOMEHOW, they managed to keep up a conversation about food for over an hour. And by the time Juliette's cell phone rang, he knew everything from her favorite kind of pizza—if anyone had asked him to guess, he would've said she preferred ones topped with veggies, not sausage—to the fact she refused to eat lamb. While she took the call, he added two more pieces of wood to the fire and made them both more tea. Her phone call didn't last long, though, because by the time he returned with their drinks, her cell phone was on the end table, and she was petting Clifford. As he predicted, as soon as she'd sat down on the sofa earlier, the dog had jumped up next to her.

Once they'd exhausted the topic of food, he'd asked if she played chess. For his birthday years ago, his parents had purchased him a beautiful marble chess set. Since until a few months ago, he'd spent his entire adult life living alone, he didn't get many chances to use it. Honestly, it'd probably gotten more use in the past seven months while he'd been teaching his niece to play than in the almost ten years he'd owned it. Perhaps at a loss for a conversation topic as well, she'd immediately agreed. They'd been playing ever since.

Whatever else he might think about Juliette, she was a damn good chess player.

"You were right about Clifford. With him around, you never need a blanket." She ran her hand down the dog's back again. Since Juliette had been there, he'd left his spot on the sofa next to her only once.

"He's a decent vacuum too. If food falls off a plate, he'll get it before it hits the floor." Aaron studied the board for a moment and then looked up. "How about we take a break?" He always struggled to concentrate when he was hungry, and thanks to his empty stomach and the beautiful woman across from him, his head wasn't on their game. "I can make us some dinner, and then we can finish the game after we eat."

While he was up, he'd get out some flashlights and candles. The sunlight streaming through the windows gave them enough light to see for the moment, but the sun would be setting soon.

Aaron didn't wait for an answer before he stood up. Even if she wasn't ready to eat a meal, he'd get himself a snack from the kitchen to hold him over.

She unfolded her legs, and in response, Clifford, who had been using her thigh as a pillow, opened his eyes. "Sounds like a plan." She came to her feet. As if that was some kind of cue, the dog jumped down and started wagging his tail. More than likely, he hoped some food was in his immediate future. The dog often thought more with his stomach than the organ in his head.

Without a word, Juliette followed him down to the kitchen. Of course, he didn't need her to say anything to know she was there. His body somehow knew she stood close enough that if he turned, he'd be able to touch her. And if he touched her, he might try to kiss her. Who knew where that might lead, especially since they had the house to themselves.

When he woke up, having a guest for dinner hadn't been

on his agenda. If it had been, he would've thawed out some chicken or pork chops. "We don't have too many options."

Before he did anything else, he took out the rechargeable lantern he kept under the kitchen sink. Although it was still at least an hour until sunset, shadows filled the room, and he saw heavy clouds moving in over the lake. Switching the device on to its lowest setting—unless pitch-black outside, the highest option was far too bright—he set it on the counter. Canned soup and pasta were two things he always kept on hand since both were quick and easy to make. He'd had pasta and meatballs last night and would rather not have it again.

"We've got plenty of canned soup and sandwich meat."

"Sounds good. What can I do to help?"

Slapping together a sandwich and heating soup didn't require much effort, and it wasn't a two-person job. "Don't worry about it. What kind of soup do you want? We've got chicken noodle, beef barley, and tomato."

"Chicken is fine."

Once he had the soup heating on the stove, he got out everything to make sandwiches. His mom always insisted guests got served first, and at some point in his life, he'd adopted her theory. "What kind of sandwich would you like?"

Juliette's hand covered his as he reached for the bread. Heat hotter than the flame under the saucepan on the stove shot across his skin. "I can make the sandwiches for us. Just tell me what you want."

You. "A little of everything. And while you take care of this, I'll get some flashlights and candles from the garage."

Maybe while he was out there, he'd find his common sense too, because the more time he spent around Juliette, the more he wanted to take his sister's advice and see what happened if he asked her out.

When he came back, two sandwiches sat on the counter, and Juliette stood at the stove mixing the chicken soup.

Although he'd seen her in his kitchen several times, he'd never noticed just how right she looked there, as if she actually belonged, which was bizarre because in another two months or so, she'd check out and they'd never see her again.

"I lowered the heat because it was boiling."

"Thanks." *She's not sticking around.* He sent himself the mental reminder and got out two bowls. "If you want to get something to drink or start eating, I'll take care of this." He waited for her to move so he could fill the bowls. Rather than move away, she turned off the stove, removed the bowls from his hands, and set them down.

Stepping closer, she met his eyes and gestured toward the stack of magazines on the counter that hadn't made it into the recycling bin. Even without looking, he knew her face graced the cover of the one on top. He also remembered the headline above the picture.

"I didn't know he was married."

Okay, did she expect a response from him? And if so, what kind? He parted his lips, although he had no idea what he planned to say. He didn't get a chance to speak, however.

"The media is claiming otherwise. But I wanted you to know the truth. If I'd known Daniel was married, I never would've gotten involved with him."

For the second time in the space of a few seconds, she left him scrambling for a response. "That's...."

The signals traveling from his brain to his mouth paused when Juliette took a step closer to him, and her breasts brushed against his chest. Since his move back to Avon, he hadn't spent a lot of time around women, but he recognized the intent on Juliette's face. Aaron should move away, put a little breathing room between them. The hand suddenly on his shoulder kept him in place better than the concrete blocks he used to keep the swim platform in place in the lake.

Any neurons still firing in his brain stopped when her lips

touched his. And every reason he'd given himself for not getting involved with Juliette evaporated as she caressed his lips with hers.

Sooner than he would've liked, she pulled her mouth away, but her hand remained on the back of his neck. Exactly when it got there, he couldn't say, but her fingers continued to move across his skin much the way her lips had been moving against his a second ago. Unfortunately, the nerve endings on his neck seemed to be the only things working at the damn moment. His head certainly wasn't—at least not the head on top of his shoulders. The one below his belt certainly had some ideas. Ones he had no intention of letting happen tonight.

CHAPTER 8

OVER THE YEARS, Juliette had spent enough time around men to know when one was interested in her. Today as they discussed their favorite foods and played chess, she used the opportunity to watch Aaron. He'd quickly told her everything she needed to know for the moment.

She'd always believed waiting for someone else to take charge was a waste of time. That applied to both life in general as well as romantic relationships. So despite her earlier insistence that getting involved with a man right now was a bad idea, she made the first move and kissed him.

She'd shocked the hell out of him too. When her lips first touched his, she'd felt his whole body tense up. Even after he relaxed enough to participate in the kiss, he hadn't tried to take control of it; instead, all he'd done was put a hand on her waist. A lot of men liked to be in control of everything from kissing to making love. Daniel had been that way. He always needed to set the pace and intensity when they kissed. She much preferred a man who didn't mind sharing the driver's seat. Her instincts told her Aaron would share no matter what activity they engaged in. Not that she wanted to engage in anything other than some more kissing tonight. But she was going to be here for a least another two months, maybe even longer depending on what happened with the old dance studio. A lot could happen in two months.

Moving away, she slowly let her hand fall away from his neck. "I didn't come here looking to meet anyone."

Honesty from the beginning made everything easier in the long run. Too bad Daniel hadn't believed the same thing. If he'd told her from the start he was married, she would've said "nice to meet you, but I don't date married men" and kept on walking.

"Actually, a big part of the reason I came was to get away from that." She pointed over her shoulder toward the offending magazine. "But things change."

Aaron nodded and leaned his hip against the counter. "And let me guess, you want to know if I have any friends I can introduce you to." Laughter twinkled in his eyes, but somehow he managed to maintain a serious expression.

Hey, if he wanted to have a little fun and tease her, she'd give it right back to him. "Exactly. Wow, it's like you read my mind. Do you have any friends I might enjoy spending time with? And just so you know, I'm partial to ones with dark hair and green eyes."

His gaze dropped to her lips for a heartbeat or two before meeting hers. "I might."

In one fluid motion, he pulled away from the counter and closed the distance between them again. Aaron lowered his lips toward hers far too slowly, but she resisted the urge to initiate their second kiss. She'd let him have control this time around.

"I'll let you know later," he said just before his mouth touched hers.

Off in the distance, she heard her cell phone ring. She ignored it because nothing except perhaps aliens landing in the kitchen would get her to move from this spot and put an end to their kiss, which, although closed-mouth, was making her a little weak in the knees. She'd been kissed by a lot of men—perhaps too many—but this, well, this was different. It was like all those other guys had been kissers in the minor league while Aaron was the major league's star player. If he kissed this well, how did he perform in other areas?

Pulling away, he touched her cheek as he looked at her. "I think I heard your phone."

She'd never been left speechless by a kiss. Clearly, there was a first time even for that, so she nodded.

"Do you want to go and check it? I can finish getting dinner ready while you do."

Unless the call was from her sister or brother telling her aliens from Mars had landed on Earth, she didn't care who had called or what they wanted. And since scientists had never found evidence of aliens living on any planet in their solar system, she doubted the phone call had anything to do with Martians or any other space dwellers.

"Nah, I'll check it later. Let's eat before the soup gets cold." *And then maybe you can further showcase your kissing skills.*

The fingers on her cheek slipped away, and he reached for a bowl. "If you want to grab us something to drink, I'll take care of this."

"I can handle that. What do you want?"

"Get me whatever you're having."

When she sat down across from him, he thanked her for the water before digging into his meal. With his attention focused on his food, she turned hers to the bowl in front of her. She didn't eat soup often, but when she did, it didn't come out of a can with a shelf life of probably years. But at least she had a hot meal, and really, how bad could it be?

She alternated between bites of her sandwich and her

soup, which turned out to be far better than she'd expected but worlds away from what Paulette prepared. Aaron, on the other hand, polished off his soup before pulling the plate with his sandwich closer to him. Why his eating behavior fascinated her, she didn't know, but it did. Maybe it was merely because the man himself held her interest. Even if no one told her anything else about him, the fact he'd invited his sister and niece to live with him told her how much he valued family. His rescue of her today also suggested a streak of chivalry lingered inside him, a trait she'd never found in any of the men she'd dated. Actually, she doubted most even knew what the word meant.

But she wanted to know more.

What were his favorite movies? Did he prefer the winter or the summer? Did he have any favorite authors or movies? While she might have been able to discover those things from his sister or even his mom, she wanted to spend time with him and get answers to all her questions.

And who could blame her? The guy had opened his house to a woman he barely knew because she was cold, looked great in a pair of jeans, and kissed like a master.

"How often do you drive into Boston?" The only way she'd get to know him better was by spending more time with him after today.

He lowered the hand holding his sandwich and swallowed the food in his mouth. "Usually a couple of times a month. I was there last week, so most likely, I won't go back until sometime in April."

"Then, you'll be around this week?"

Aaron nodded and took another bite from his sandwich.

If she was at home or even at her parents' house, she could come up with a nice long list of places they could go and things they could do. Here, she had no idea. If the little of the town she'd seen was a good indication, there wasn't much to do in Avon outside of hiking and using the lake. And at the moment it was too warm for ice skating and the water was far too cold for swimming, so that narrowed down her options even more. Still, when she wanted something, she went after it. Right now, she wanted to get to know Aaron—or as he should be known, The Master Kisser —better.

"I'm waiting to hear back from Caryn Ferguson. She's supposed to set up some appointments for me this week."

"The real estate agent?"

She should have known Aaron would know who Caryn Ferguson was. According to the internet search she'd done, the woman owned the only real estate office in town. "Mmm. I called her yesterday."

He placed the last of his sandwich back on the plate rather than eat it. "You're thinking about buying a house in town?"

She could've just told him she had proof aliens existed, and he wouldn't have looked or sounded more surprised.

That's usually why people contact real estate agents. Sometimes a conversation called for sarcasm, and other times it didn't. Right now, it didn't strike her as one of those times. "I haven't decided 100 percent, but yes. I'm also going to look at the building where Dance Dynamics used to be."

She hadn't shared her idea of opening a dance school and moving to Avon for at least part of the year with a single person. She hadn't felt any need or desire to since, at the end of the day, it was her life and her money. Now she not only wanted to share her possible plans with Aaron but sensed she needed to.

Resting his elbows on the table, he laced his fingers together. His expression gave her no clear indication of what thoughts were churning inside his head. And she wanted to know.

"So, you came here to get away from the media, and now

you're thinking about moving to town and opening a business."

Well, when someone put it that way, it sounded nutty. But then again, the media hadn't been her only reason for leaving New York. She'd also hoped to make some decisions about her future while away from her day-to-day life.

"Have you ever known you needed a change but not been sure what kind?"

His shoulders moved a fraction of an inch. "Yeah, I guess."

"That's how I've been for months now." She'd never be able to explain it, but she found finally sharing her feelings with Aaron oddly liberating. "When Holly suggested Avon, it sounded like a good place to avoid the media and figure a few things out. I've always loved to dance. In high school, I got accepted to study it at Juilliard."

"You got in and didn't go. Isn't Juilliard the Harvard for the performing arts?"

Juliette had never heard anyone describe it as such, but it was a good analogy. "My parents convinced me I'd be better off getting some kind of business-related degree, so I majored in marketing and minored in dance at Columbia. If I hadn't already started modeling, they probably wouldn't have been able to change my mind. But I'd been after my parents for years to let me get into it, and at the time, I enjoyed it almost as much as dancing. So, I caved and went where they wanted me to. I'm not sure who was more surprised when I did, my parents or me."

She'd never shared any of that with anyone outside of her family. Not even Holly, who she'd known for years, knew she'd declined acceptance to Juilliard and done what her parents wanted.

"Can't say I blame your parents. The job market for professional dancers isn't huge. Not that you—" Aaron cleared his throat and reached for his drink. "—should've done what they wanted," he said after he swallowed his water.

It could've been what he'd intended to say before going for his glass. The way he didn't quite meet her eyes hinted it wasn't. And she had a good idea of what words had been on his tongue before he stopped himself.

"You're right. And if I hadn't been able to find a job after graduating, I would've been fine. But in my family, it isn't acceptable to lounge around and do nothing. My brother, Scott, works for Sherbrooke Enterprises, and my sister, Courtney, works for the Helping Hands Foundation in Providence. It's the same with my cousins."

He shifted uncomfortably in his chair, but his eyes met hers as he covered her hand with his. "I didn't mean to insult you."

It'd been a logical assumption on his part. She knew several people who had graduated from Phillips Academy with her and then gone on to Harvard or Columbia but now did nothing but spend money, travel, and party. Eventually, a few might move into the corporate world and take over the various companies their relatives had built, but until the need arose, no one expected anything from them.

Intending to kiss the frown off his face, she leaned toward him. "You didn't."

As tempting as she found the idea of teasing his lips apart and finding out what other parts of her body might get affected by a more intense kiss, she kept this one short and sweet. Later, when they finished dinner and moved to a slightly more comfortable location, though, she'd indulge. She didn't anticipate getting any complaints from him either when she did.

∾

NOT LONG AFTER sticking his size eleven foot his mouth, he'd finished the last of his sandwich, and they'd cleared the table together. He told her not to worry about it and suggested she return to the living room, by far the warmest place in the house. However, she'd insisted on helping. Even before he walked into her cottage earlier today, he'd suspected his initial opinion of her might have been a little off. Unlike some of the wealthy city guests they'd had in the past, she never called the office and complained. She was always friendly when she joined them for dinner, and when Mom offered to do her grocery shopping, she turned her down. Not to mention, both Candace and Mom only had nice things to say about her. In general, both women were good judges of character. Hell, even Tiegan's comments about her were complimentary.

The past several hours he'd spent with her had driven home how wrong he'd been. After the power went out, she could've called and demanded firewood or extra blankets. She hadn't. Instead, she'd made the best of what she had. Later, rather than complain when he offered her canned soup and sandwiches for dinner, she'd offered to help him. Then when he'd opened his mouth and almost insulted her, she'd kissed him.

Think before you speak. Usually, he didn't need to remind himself of that. "You don't enjoy modeling anymore?" If her future plans included opening a dance studio in Northern New Hampshire, it must not hold the appeal it once did.

Juliette didn't look up as she reached for a pawn on the chessboard. Before she touched it, though, she dropped her hand back on her thigh. "Yes and no. Mostly no." She tapped her fingers against her leg as she continued to survey the board. "Pierre would flip if he heard me say that. But I've been doing it for more than ten years, and I want a change.

My mom wants me to join her and my sister at the Helping Hands Foundation."

She reached out and moved her bishop, then looked at him. "I've thought about accepting the position, mostly because it would mean I'm closer to much of my family. But I don't think it's what I want." Juliette raised her wine glass toward her mouth but spoke again before it reached its destination. "That's not true. I know it's not what I want. I think I'd go crazy sitting behind a desk all day. I'm not sure how my sister and brother manage it every day."

At the moment, he was far more interested in their conversation than the chess game. So rather than examine the board and consider his next move, he studied her as she sipped her wine. "If you want to be closer to your family, wouldn't it make more sense to open a dance studio near them?"

"Avon isn't that far from them, and I like it here. Besides, there are plenty of dance studios in Providence and Boston. Candace said the closest one to town is over an hour away, so I think a new studio would do well here."

He didn't doubt it. Every time his sister and Sandy held classes through the parks and rec department, they filled up as soon as registration opened. Add Juliette's well-known name to the already high demand for a new school, and she'd have no problem keeping the business afloat.

"I also really like the people I've met in town."

Unfolding her legs and setting down her glass, she moved closer to him on the sofa, disturbing Clifford who had fallen asleep against her side. As if some doggy sixth sense kicked in telling Clifford to give them some privacy, he jumped to the floor and curled up closer to the woodstove. Later, he'd have to give the dog an extra treat.

"Especially one." The fingers that moments ago held her chess piece traced his jaw before slipping around the back of his neck. Once there, they brushed across his skin, leaving a trail of goose bumps in their wake. What would happen if she brushed her fingers across other areas? Hopefully, he'd find out before she left town.

"Anyone I know?" Unlike women he'd dated in the past, Juliette didn't wait for him to make the first move. He liked that. Far more than he'd ever thought he would.

She slipped her other hand over his shoulder and pressed a gentle kiss on his neck. "Possibly." She moved her lips higher and kissed his jaw. "And I want to get to know him better." This time her lips brushed against the corner of his mouth. "Assuming he's interested in spending time with me."

Before he uttered an answer, Juliette claimed his lips. Each pass of her mouth across his clouded his thoughts, pushing aside everything but the feel of her against him. In the kitchen, he'd let her keep the reins when she kissed him; right now he didn't feel like being led.

Before she could do anything else, he traced her bottom lip with the tip of his tongue. On cue, she opened for him. His senses reeled as if struck by lightning when his tongue touched hers. Soon he no longer knew who was in control. And he didn't care. The only thing that mattered was that the kiss didn't end anytime soon.

His brain was too far gone to know whether she broke away first or he did. Slowly, his ability to form words returned, as did the knowledge that Juliette wasn't like other women he dated. Yeah, it appeared as though his initial opinion of her had been wrong, but he didn't want to rush into a relationship with her either—that was if she even wanted a relationship. She might just want a sexual partner while in Avon. While not opposed to the idea, he needed more than a single meal with a woman before sleeping with her. If you could even call canned soup and sandwiches a meal. The balance in his bank account didn't even come close to hers, but he could treat his dates to far better meals than they'd eaten tonight.

Her fingers on his neck went back to work. Or maybe they'd never stopped. He didn't know. Hell, with Juliette practically sitting in his lap, he wasn't even sure of the day of the week.

"Should I take that as a yes?" A smile pulled at the corners of her lips, ruining the serious tone of her voice.

Aaron kissed the skin just below her ear and smiled when she trembled. "Yeah, I'd say that's a safe assumption."

DURING THE OFF-SEASON, when his mom had a lot of time on her hands, she spent a decent amount of it baking. Thanks to his proximity to her, he was usually the recipient of those baked goods, a situation he rather enjoyed. Her most recent delivery was a mixed-berry pie. Although she'd only dropped it off yesterday before heading to Boston, less than half remained now thanks to his and Juliette's efforts.

"This is so good." Her lips closed around the fork, and he held back a groan at the sight.

They'd ended their marathon make-out session a good fifteen minutes ago, and his body wanted to know why he was indulging in pie rather than something far more pleasurable. Despite the erection pressing against the zipper of his jeans—one that showed no signs of going away anytime soon —he didn't regret ending their previous activity before they went any farther.

Before he thought better of it, he tucked several strands of hair behind her ear. Thanks to his fingers, the neat ponytail she'd had before was a bit of a loose mess, with more hair out of the band holding it back than in it. And now that he'd touched her again, he wanted to kiss her. If he did that at the moment, he might not be able to stop without seeing just how far she'd let him go.

And that wasn't him.

Aaron always waited until he knew a woman better before becoming intimate with her, no matter how attracted he was to her. Sometimes it was easier than other times. But nothing like tonight. Rather than spend time getting to know Juliette the person, he wanted to lay her on the floor by the fire, strip her naked, and get to know her body better. Then worry about getting to know everything else about her later.

Food. The topic saved him earlier. Maybe it'd help him out again. "It's even better heated with some vanilla ice cream."

"Or maybe whipped cream."

An image what else might be delectable covered in whipped cream popped up as he met her eyes. The camping lantern on the table provided sufficient lighting, and her expression hinted that she knew exactly where his thoughts had gone.

Is she trying to torture me? Before he suggested they get out a can and use it, he gulped down the rest of his wine. "Ice cream is much better." He refilled his glass before adding more to hers.

"Next time we have pie, we'll have to try both and then decide." With a smile, she took a sip from her glass. "Since you're not going into Boston this week, does that mean you're free at night?"

"Mondays I usually stay here with Tiegan while Candace is at class. But I don't have any plans for the rest of the week." He didn't have to stay with Tiegan on Mondays either. His mom could do it, but unless he was traveling for work like earlier this month or in Boston, he handled Monday nights, and his mom covered Wednesdays.

"Good. Then maybe we can do something on Tuesday."

She'd rented all the available cottages and, as far as he knew, hadn't ventured even into the grocery store. He might be wrong, but that told him she didn't want anyone to know she was in Avon. If they went to George's Diner or the movies, it wouldn't be long before everyone knew she was visiting town. She must know that. Then again, as soon as Caryn Ferguson started showing her homes, half the town would know Juliette was staying at the campground anyway. Caryn might be a top-notch real estate agent, but she liked to be the center of attention, a trait the agent had passed on to her daughter, a woman Aaron had known since preschool. Telling everyone she'd not only met but was helping supermodel Juliette Belmont find a home would provide Caryn with the limelight, if even just for a little while.

"Yeah, sure."

If possible, the smile she gave him brightened the room more than the lantern on the table.

"When we're done eating, if you want to call it a night, I'll get you some blankets from upstairs. If you'd rather use my bedroom, you can, and I'll sleep on the sofa. I can go up and change the sheets, but it won't be as warm as the living room." He had a fourth unoccupied bedroom upstairs; however, it lacked a bed. Instead, his sister used it as a place to study.

"Down here is fine. But I'm not ready for bed yet. We haven't finished our chess game."

Chess took a certain level of concentration, something he didn't have. After the way they'd kissed earlier, he hoped she didn't either. If she did, he'd done something wrong and needed to rectify the situation.

Securing his arms around her, he moved onto his back and brought her down on top of him. "Let's finish it tomorrow." Tonight he wanted to focus whatever brain activity he had left on her.

CHAPTER 9

OPENING HIS EYES, Aaron stared at the ceiling, momentarily confused by why he didn't see the ceiling fan above him. Then the reason for the missing fan came to him. He was in the living room, not his bedroom. More specifically, he was in a sleeping bag on the living room floor.

He could've gone upstairs last night and spent a far more comfortable evening in his bed. If he'd been alone, he more than likely would've done that after putting out the fire in the woodstove and then rekindled it in the morning if he needed it. And if his usual housemates had been there, he would've slept on the sofa so the fire in the woodstove wasn't unattended while they retreated upstairs and slept in their beds and benefited from the heat rising to the upper level of the house. But last night he hadn't been alone, and his niece and sister weren't the ones keeping him company. Although he'd never had any issues with the woodstove, he didn't want to leave a fire going while he went upstairs, and Juliette remained down here. If it had been his sister on the sofa, he would've considered it. Candace had grown up using the woodstove, and more importantly, he knew how she'd react in case of an emergency. For all he knew, this was the first time his current guest had ever used anything but central heating for warmth. Rather than take any unnecessary risks, he'd dug his sleeping bag out and slept downstairs on the floor. Not surprisingly, his dog slept in one of the overstuffed armchairs rather than join him. Aaron didn't blame him. And if there'd been any way for him to fit his entire body on a chair, he would've too, because the chair was far more comfortable than the hardwood floor.

Is the power back? He hoped so. He enjoyed the outdoors and camping as much as anyone, but going without electricity when you chose to sleep in a tent was one thing. At times like this, it was altogether different. Not to mention the fact that his niece hated the dark, and she'd be home tomorrow. Every night, she slept with a nightlight, the brightest one he'd ever seen, turned on. And since they'd moved in with him, they hadn't lost power for more than an hour or two, and never when it affected Tiegan going to bed. If bedtime rolled around tomorrow night and she couldn't use it, he didn't know what she would do. Then, of course, there was his current house guest to consider. She hadn't complained yesterday, but it'd been clear she wasn't used to roughing it in the least.

Rather than get up and find out if the lights worked, Aaron readjusted the pillow under his head and turned his thoughts to the previous evening—or, more specifically, to what had transpired starting at dinnertime and ending before he climbed into his sleeping bag.

If someone had told him he'd find himself on the sofa with his lip pressed against hers and Juliette's hands under his shirt caressing his skin, he would've laughed in their face. But he'd spent a portion of his night in just such a position. When their lips hadn't been touching, they'd talked. He didn't recall all of their conversations, but he remembered her telling him more about her plans to purchase a home in town and open a dance school. He didn't know if she'd go through with it. She might spend some time looking at property and realize she couldn't handle spending more than a few weeks in Avon. If she did, he couldn't blame her.

He loved the town, but once in a while even he found it too small and, well, dull. And he'd lived here much of his life. Juliette lived in New York City, arguably one of the busiest cities in the world. Regardless of the time or the day of the week, a person could find something to do there. Here, even at noon on a Saturday, it could be tough to find a way to occupy your time, especially during the cold winter months.

Whatever happens, happens. Juliette might wake up this morning, turn in her key to the cottage, and head back to New York, especially if faced with another day of no hot water. If she did, he'd have some pleasant memories from last night, and his life would go on.

Thud. Aaron bolted upright at the sound, and all thoughts of what Juliette might do vanished.

"Ouch." The word quickly followed the sound.

"Are you okay?" He'd left his flannel pajama bottoms and T-shirt on when he climbed into his sleeping bag last night, so he didn't need to worry about pulling on clothes after he stood. Even still, Clifford reached her side before he did.

"Yeah." She moved into a sitting position on the floor and scratched the dog near his collar.

In his thirty-four years, he'd never been jealous of a dog until now. Instead of giving his dog attention, he wanted her to be giving him some more of the attention she'd given him yesterday. "Are you sure?" He knelt on the floor next to her.

"I fell off the sofa, not Mount Everest. I'm fine. Really." She blew some hair away from her face and moved back to her original location on the sofa. "I'm used to having a little more room at night."

Aaron sat down next to her before his dog got any ideas and jumped into the spot—something the furry guy would do in a heartbeat if it meant a belly rub or scratch behind the ears.

He hadn't heard her during the night, but that didn't mean she'd had a great sleep either. "Other than your unpleasant wake-up call, did you sleep okay?" He'd slept on the sofa a few times. While not as comfortable as his bed upstairs, he'd slept on far worse in hotel rooms.

"Didn't wake up once. How about you?"

He'd woken up a handful of times to check on the fire but had fallen back to sleep quickly. "Not bad."

Curious whether he could make some coffee or if he'd have to settle for tea again, Aaron tried the lamp on the table. It didn't surprise him when nothing happened. When they spoke yesterday, Robby had told him not to expect power back anytime soon.

"Looks like coffee is out this morning. Do you want some tea? Or hot chocolate." Next time he went to the store, maybe he should pick up some instant coffee. He preferred even the instant stuff to hot tea.

Juliette brushed her lips against his cheek, waking him up better than any caffeinated beverage ever would. "Tea, please."

Standing up, she stretched her arms over her head, and the hem of her shirt rose several inches, exposing a strip of flesh. And as if she'd waved a magic wand, the erection he'd gone to bed with returned. Before he gave in to the temptation and checked to see if the skin on display was as soft as the skin on her arms, he clenched his hands into fists.

"I'll meet you in the kitchen," she said, dropping her arms to her sides and removing the temptation from view.

He watched her walk away. Even dressed in a pair of knit pajama bottoms and a New England Rebels sweatshirt, she had the power to make him feel like a fifteen-year-old who'd never had sex. If she ever tried to turn him on, he might not survive.

Aaron pushed himself off the sofa. As if he knew where Aaron intended to go, Clifford jumped to the floor and took a few steps toward the hall. "You've got a one-track mind there, my friend."

Then again, some might say the same thing about him. Yep, his thoughts, including his dreams last night, had focused on nothing but Juliette since her lips touched his yesterday.

Liar. Even before they'd kissed, she had starring roles in several of his dreams.

JULIETTE HEARD her cell phone ring while washing her face, so before heading to the kitchen, she made a pit stop back in the living room. A quick look at the screen showed she had two voice mail messages.

She played the message from Curt first. In it, he explained that, like much of the state, Pelham didn't have any power, but his house had a generator, so she was more than welcome to come and stay with him until things returned to normal. She'd call him back later after she decided whether to take him up on the offer. If electricity didn't return sometime today, she'd rather not return to her icebox of a cottage. At the same time, she didn't know if Aaron would want her spending another night here. And even if he offered her another night on the sofa, she didn't want to abuse his kindness.

The second voice mail, the one she'd received last night, was from her mom. They hadn't spoken in about a week, but like with the first message, Juliette didn't feel any immediate need to return the call. She also found a text message from

Holly waiting for her. According to the time stamp, it'd come in around eight last night, but she hadn't heard the distinct chime she set for when she received texts. Then again, she'd been pleasantly occupied much of the evening. And if left up to her, she'd be busy in much the same manner for part of today.

Rather than ignore the message, she typed a short reply promising to call later as she walked toward the kitchen.

When she reached the doorway, she stopped. Aaron stood at the counter slicing up fresh strawberries. Two coffee mugs were set out just waiting to be filled with hot water. And behind him, a teakettle sat on the stove, a slight stream of steam escaping from it, suggesting that the water would be boiling soon.

"Since I'm already boiling water, I'm making oatmeal for breakfast. We have some fresh fruit too." He looked up from his task. "But if you don't want that, I can make you eggs."

Had a man ever cooked her breakfast? She didn't remember any. Of course, she doubted many of her past boyfriends knew how to turn on a stove, let alone cook even something as simple as oatmeal.

Boyfriend? Could she assign the term to the man in front of her? They'd kissed, but she didn't consider every man she kissed a boyfriend. She'd carried on with a man much the way she had with Aaron last night and then never saw him again. And she'd had a few one-night stands, although there were very few people she'd ever share that information with. So nothing about the night before guaranteed a relationship between her and Aaron loomed on the horizon. And just because he stood there cooking breakfast didn't mean he wanted her around all day. What had taken place between them last night could've been a way for him to pass the time, since watching television was impossible. At this very moment, he might be slicing strawberries and praying the power switched on so he could show her the door and then turn on a movie or basketball game.

Her intuition told her otherwise though. Aaron didn't come across as the type to engage in any kind of intimacy simply because he needed a way to pass the time. No, she sensed he would've suggested they get back to their chess game after dinner to occupy their time instead.

She hadn't come up here looking for any type of relationship or even wanting one. But she hadn't expected to meet Aaron, a man who sliced up strawberries for her to eat with breakfast and slept on the floor so she could have the sofa.

"Oatmeal sounds good." She came around the counter and snagged a strawberry slice off the plate. "Anything I can do to help?" She popped the berry in her mouth. Before she could lick the lingering juice off her fingers, Aaron reached for her hand.

"Nah, I'm all set," he said, raising her hand to his mouth and sucking the juice off her index finger. He held her gaze as he did the same with her middle finger.

Well, she doubted he wanted her to leave so he could watch television. In the living room, her bladder had stopped her from giving him the type of kiss she wanted. That no longer remained an issue. Slipping an arm around his waist, she kissed the right corner of his mouth. Then she kissed the other side.

"I don't think I said good morning." Juliette pulled her face away from his just enough to see his eyes. She found a unique combination of humor and heat reflecting back at her.

Aaron shook his head. "Your first word this morning was 'ouch.'" He settled a hand on either side of her waist and aligned their bodies against each other. Then he smiled. And if she'd had a fan handy, she would've used it as a wave of heat and excitement zapped her all the way to her painted toenails.

She moistened her suddenly dry lips and attempted to form words. "Well, good morning." Rather than touch her mouth to his, she ran her tongue along his bottom lip before pressing her open lips against his.

Home. The word fluttered through her thoughts like a butterfly in a flower garden. She couldn't explain it, but right then, it was as if she'd been waiting for this man to come into her life. As if she belonged in Aaron's arms, kissing him, and not anywhere else.

The whistling kettle cut through the silence in the room, and she'd never hated an inanimate object more than just then.

Slowly, he pulled back. "Remember where we were so we can finish later."

Oh, she'd remember, no question about it. She'd also spend some time later processing whatever she'd just felt. She'd experienced excitement and lust while kissing a man enough to recognize it. While both emotions had been present just now, an entirely new and unique emotion had trumped both.

Nodding, she latched on to the first thing that came to her mind as well as the counter for support, because her knees were a tad unsteady. "Do you mind if I get some milk for my tea?"

Turning off the stove, Aaron poured the boiling water into each cup. "Of course not. Help yourself to whatever is in there." At the counter, he added water to the bowls of oatmeal before setting the teakettle back on the stove. "While you're in there, can you grab the maple syrup and strawberry jam?"

Juliette grabbed the milk, the items Aaron requested, and the container of fresh blueberries, since he'd told her to get whatever she wanted. She rarely passed on any kind of fresh fruit, and blueberries were her all-time favorite. "Do you know what time everyone will be home?"

After depositing the cereal bowls and teas on the table, he went back for the bread. "Sometime tomorrow," he answered as he pulled a jar of peanut butter from a cabinet. "I'm surprised Candace didn't tell you."

Well, at least she didn't need to worry about them being suddenly interrupted if they picked up where they left off last night. "Tomorrow is Monday. Doesn't Tiegan have school?"

"Nope. The teachers have workshops." Aaron sat down next to her and started making a peanut butter and strawberry jam sandwich to go along with his oatmeal. "That's one of the reasons I got the tickets for this weekend instead of next. I figured the three of them could stay longer in Boston and have fun." He slapped the two slices of bread together. "It's been a rough year for my sister and niece. But in a lot of ways, I think it's been worse for Tiegan, so I wanted to make sure she enjoyed her birthday."

She resisted the urge to lean over and kiss him. Other than the male members of her family, she couldn't recall ever meeting a man who valued family as much as she did until now.

He gestured toward the sandwich with his knife. "Do you want one?"

"I'm all set." She'd eaten peanut butter sandwiches for lunch and breakfast yesterday, so she'd pass on one this morning. She watched him pour maple syrup on his oatmeal before adding a spoonful of strawberries. She'd never tried it that way, but it looked tasty, so she added a little to hers too. "Where are they staying?"

She didn't stay in the city often. Until the past year or so, she'd had two relatives living in Boston, and her parents' home in Weston wasn't that far away either. On the rare occasion she opted for a hotel room rather than a bed owned by a family member, she had a list of preferred hotels depending on the reason for her time in Boston. If she went to see a show at the Opera House, which was where the Boston Ballet performed, she liked to stay at the Sherbrooke Park Plaza. Built in 1910, it was the oldest Sherbrooke hotel remaining in the city, although not the first constructed there. Although it'd been renovated numerous times over the years, it maintained the elegance of a building constructed at the beginning of the twentieth century. Plus, it was less than half a mile from the theatre.

Of course, she'd caught him with a mouthful of food. While she waited for an answer, she added milk and sugar to her tea, then tried her oatmeal. The maple syrup gave the oatmeal just the right hint of flavor, making an otherwise rather bland breakfast food sweet but nothing like the sugary cereals marketed to children—the very type her brother-in-law Josh loved and kept in the house.

Aaron washed his sandwich down with tea before he answered. "The Adams Hotel over on Exeter Street. It had mostly four-and-five-star ratings and an indoor pool. When I talked to Candace yesterday, she said it was quite nice." He took another sip of tea before he continued. "I tried to book something at the Sherbrooke Park Plaza because it's a little closer, but the prices for a family suite for three nights were a little too steep."

She parted her lips, prepared to tell him next time he wanted a room at the Sherbrooke Park Plaza or any other hotel owned by Sherbrooke Enterprises just to let her know when and for how long. She shoved another spoonful of oatmeal in her mouth instead of issuing her offer to take care of it for him. Although he knew what family she belonged to, he didn't bring it up or seem to treat her any differently because of it. She'd prefer to keep it that way. All too often, people either bent over backward to please her or tried to get close to her because of either her societal connections or her contacts in the modeling industry. Even the creep Daniel had inquired about whether she knew certain individuals, and when she admitted she did, he'd hinted at how he'd like an introduction.

"What do you think the chances are we'll get power back today?"

"No idea. I can try calling my friend Robby later. But he might not answer. He's probably been out working on the lines since early yesterday."

"My cousin Curt lives about two hours from here. He left me a message this morning inviting me to stay with him until everything is back to normal. I will call him after we finish breakfast."

"By the time you get there, we might have electricity back."

"Maybe, or it could be another whole day."

He lowered his overflowing spoon back to his bowl. "You're welcome to stay again tonight if it's not back on." Aaron trailed his knuckles along her jaw. The tenderness in his eyes had her wondering where he'd been all her life. "It's up to you, but I'd like you to stay."

No sane woman would be able to say no to that. Somehow words seemed inadequate, so she leaned forward and kissed him instead.

CHAPTER 10

THANKFULLY, unlike the previous day, a tumble off the sofa and onto the floor hadn't woken Juliette up. An insistent nose nudging her in the leg had. Of the two methods, she preferred the dog's way. Once she gave Clifford the attention he wanted, she followed the scent of vanilla into the kitchen, where she found Aaron once again preparing them breakfast. Although this time instead of oatmeal and fruit, he served her perhaps the best french toast she'd eaten in a long time. She was almost through her second cup of coffee and down to her last slice of french toast when Candace and Tiegan walked in the house.

Although Candace's expression revealed her curiosity, she greeted Juliette with a smile and then helped herself to coffee without asking any questions. Tiegan did the exact opposite. The first thing out of her mouth was to ask if Uncle Aaron had had a sleepover because there was a sleeping bag on the floor and blankets on the sofa. Tiegan didn't give Aaron a chance to answer before telling Juliette that when her friends slept over, they usually camped out in the living room so they could watch television and get snacks from the kitchen. When she finally gave him a chance to explain the reason for the items in the other room, Tiegan asked if she could invite a friend to sleep over tonight. In the girl's own words, it had been a super long time since she had a friend spend the night. Unsurprisingly, Candace reminded Tiegan she had school tomorrow, and sleepovers weren't allowed on school nights. Before Tiegan could argue or complain, Aaron's sister gave her daughter permission to invite a friend to stay that weekend.

Satisfied with her mom's offer, Tiegan proceeded to talk about her time in Boston and, more specifically, the show she'd attended with her mom and grandmother. Juliette realized several things while listening to her describe everything from the inside of the theater to the dancers' costumes. One, it'd been far too long since she attended the ballet or any other show for that matter, and she needed to rectify that soon. It also drove home how much she truly missed dancing.

And by the time she left Aaron's house and drove back to her cottage, she no longer sat on the fence in regard to opening a dance studio in town. Nope, she had one leg already on the other side and touching the ground. If she moved ahead with the idea, she'd be back to doing something she loved while at the same time giving children like Tiegan, who loved dance as much as she did, a place to study. As far as she saw it, if she went ahead with her plan, it'd be a win-win for everyone. Her plan would also make it much easier to pursue a relationship with Aaron—an endeavor she looked forward to in a way she never had with any other man she'd met. And judging by the time they'd spent together over the past two days, he shared her interest.

Unlocking the door, Juliette stepped inside. When she'd left on Saturday, the interior temperature had hovered around fifty degrees. Now, though, the thermostat claimed the temperature was almost at sixty-seven. Even better, she had hot water, and that meant she could take a shower—something she hadn't done since Friday. So rather than unpack her bag or make any of the phone calls she wanted to, she stepped in the tub and turned the hot water on full blast. She didn't leave until her fingertips resembled prunes either.

Showered and dressed, she grabbed her cell phone and got comfortable on the sofa, one she was glad she didn't need to sleep on tonight. Two nights spent on Aaron's had been more than enough.

It beat sleeping on the floor, she reminded herself, pulling the throw blanket over her legs and calling Holly, the first person on her mental list.

Last night, she'd told Aaron he didn't need to sleep downstairs with her. After watching him tend the fire all day, she felt confident she could keep an eye on it during the night. On the rare chance an emergency arose, she'd insisted she could wake him if she couldn't handle whatever it was. He'd turned down her offer in a manner so diplomatic, ambassadors at the United Nations would have been impressed. He'd started by explaining that he always stayed in the living room if he kept a fire burning all night. Then he went on to say that he didn't even leave the task to his sister. While she believed the first part, Juliette assumed there was only a 10 percent chance the second statement was true. In her opinion, it was far more likely Aaron worried he wouldn't have a house standing in the morning if he left her alone downstairs. Whatever the actual reason behind his decision, rather than argue, she offered to sleep on the floor so he could use the sofa. He'd turned her down without even considering it. She'd suspected he would even before she made the offer. A man who offered up the use of his house, as well as his bed and cooked breakfast for you, would not turn around and make you sleep on the floor.

With the power back and the heat once again working, it was no longer an issue. And with the housing situation back to normal, she could turn her attention to a different dilemma: what the heck she and Aaron should do tomorrow night. As tempting a thought as it was, and oh, man was it tempting, they couldn't spend the entire evening sitting on this very sofa and kissing. Nope, they needed another activity for the night.

She'd been thinking about it off and on since Saturday. As of yet, not even one possibility had come to her. She needed help from someone familiar with the area. If Aaron hadn't been sitting across from her, she would've asked Candace for suggestions when she saw her earlier. Not only would she know what was available, but she knew her brother's likes and dislikes. At least, Juliette assumed she did. She certainly knew the bulk of Scott's, and the last time they'd lived in the same house, she hadn't even been old enough to drink. She could call her, but Candace had been away for the past few days and probably had things to do before heading to her class tonight.

But if Holly didn't answer, she'd have to either risk bothering Aaron's sister or maybe reach out to Holly's mom.

"Hey, I was thinking about calling you," Holly greeted after the fifth ring. "Are you still at the campground?"

"Yeah, why wouldn't I be?"

"My mom called me last night when she and dad got home from the airport. They went down to Florida to visit my aunt for her birthday."

Well, that explained why Mrs. Lambert hadn't answered when she called on Saturday morning. She'd been disappointed at the time, but now she might have to thank the woman for not being in town the next time she saw her.

"She said the power had been out since sometime Friday night. She was worried about you. I told her you'd probably left and gone to stay with your cousin or parents. Please tell me you just got back and didn't spend the weekend with no heat."

"No, I've been here the whole time."

"You must be half frozen. You should have called my brother. He would've let you stay with him. That's where Tara stayed."

She'd thought of Marc when Mrs. Lambert didn't answer on Saturday. But although she'd seen Holly's twin countless times when he'd visited her, she didn't have his phone number. "I don't have Marc's number."

"Really? You should have called me. I would've given it to you," Holly said before she rattled off Marc's number. "Seriously, if you ever need help, call him. He won't mind."

She jotted down the number and later would add it to her contact list. Even if she never called Holly's twin, it didn't hurt to have Marc's contact info.

"I can't believe you stayed there and froze your butt off. I know you wanted some time alone, but that's nuts."

Time to set the record straight so she could move the conversation on to her reason for calling. "I stayed at Aaron's house until the power came back this morning."

"Inviting you to stay there sounds like something Candace would do. When we were in school, other kids would always ask her for help because they knew she wouldn't say no. Next time I come to visit, I think I'll stop by and say hello."

Yeah, judging by the time she'd spent with Candace, she could see that happening. "She didn't invite me. Aaron did. Candace was in Boston with her daughter and mom all weekend."

"You and Aaron alone all weekend with very little to do? Tell me you found a pleasurable way to pass the time."

Juliette looked toward the ceiling. Sex was never far from her friend's mind. "Oh, yeah. We played a few games of chess, had some nice conversations about our favorite foods, and shared some meals. You get the picture. All things considered, it was a pleasant weekend." She envisioned Holly shaking her head. "Oh, and I slept on the sofa in the living room."

Several seconds of silence followed her admission. No doubt Holly was trying to determine if Juliette needed some kind of friendly intervention.

"I'm guessing it wasn't an X-rated version of chess. Like every time you lost a pawn, you had to give Aaron a lap dance or something."

An X-rated game of chess, now that was a novel idea. Maybe one that deserved future thought. "Nope. Just regular old chess."

"I know you said you didn't want to get into a relationship until the pictures of you and Daniel stop popping up, but the two of you were alone. As in, the only people in the house. No one would've known what you did to pass the time. If I'd been in your place, I wouldn't have slept on the sofa, and we wouldn't have played chess. Well, I guess if Aaron flat-out told me sex was off the table, I would have, but he's a guy. Guys don't pass on no-strings-attached sex."

Juliette disagreed. Sure, she knew plenty of men—and women, for that matter—who fit Holly's description, but she also knew some who didn't. Before Holly really got going on the subject, and Juliette knew from experience her friend would, she needed to come clean. "I didn't say we only talked and played chess."

"Details. All. The. Details."

Sometimes she shared specific details about her sex life with Holly. Other times she didn't. "We kissed."

"That's it? Did he at least kiss more than just your lips? I'd share the details with you if I'd spent the weekend with Aaron."

An image of Holly lying on the floor as Aaron moved his lips slowly down her body while his hands rested between her thighs formed. Anger and an unfamiliar emotion settled in her chest.

Hands off. The words took shape, and she took in a deep breath before speaking again. Holly was more than six hours away and hadn't seen Aaron in close to two years. She had no reason to worry.

"All I'm going to say is, the man has one talented mouth." She'd let Holly interpret that statement however she wanted. "But I didn't call to talk to you about Aaron. I need your help. I asked him out for tomorrow night. Any suggestions of where we should go?"

"Boston. Unless you go to the movies or hiking, there isn't much to do in Avon."

Perhaps some other time, they could drive into Boston and spend a night or two, but not tomorrow. "People don't sit in their houses all the time. There has to be something else around besides the movie theater."

"A mini-golf course opened last year, but it's probably still closed for the season. Silver Lanes Bowling and Lounge is over in Ashford. I haven't been to it in a long time, but they used to have a separate area with pool tables too. And Tree Ventures is in Ashford too. It's one of those outdoor rope courses. But I don't think it opens until early May."

It didn't sound like she had many options available, at least not until the weather warmed up more.

"Maybe you should take him to dinner. There are some nice restaurants in Ashford. My favorite is the Stomping

Ground. It's right on the lake. There is a nice little winery in Ashford too. Afterward, take him back to your cottage and have some fun doing something other than playing chess."

She'd already planned to feed him, although she hadn't decided if she'd try to cook for him here or venture out to a restaurant. "Thanks for the suggestions. If you think of anything else before tomorrow night, let me know."

"Will do. And call me sometime on Wednesday. I want to know how your night goes."

Oh, she'd be talking to Holly soon, because if Juliette didn't call her, Holly would reach out.

AARON FOUND Candace flipping through a magazine and drinking tea when he came back downstairs from putting away his sleeping bag and the blankets Juliette had used. She hadn't said anything about finding Juliette eating breakfast with him yet, but he'd seen the look on her face when she joined them. It was only a matter of time before she opened her mouth. If he got her talking about something else first, perhaps they'd run out of time, and she wouldn't get a chance to ask whatever questions were floating around in her head.

"Sounded like Tiegan had a lot of fun." He poured himself more coffee before taking a seat at the table. "What about you? Did you enjoy the show?"

Candace closed the magazine, revealing the photos of Juliette on the cover. One of them showed her exiting a building, perhaps where she lived. In another, she stood between a pretty brunette and a dark-haired man about his own age. A third photo of Juliette having dinner with a man completed the set. He guessed the man in the last picture was the married jerk she'd dated. He saw nothing wrong with men who chose to date a lot rather than enter into a long-term relationship. A few of his friends preferred to live their lives that way. He had a big problem with guys—women too, for that matter—who made a commitment to one person and then messed around on the side. Juliette claimed she hadn't known the jerk in the photo was married. He saw no reason not to believe her.

"Mom and I both did too. It was an amazing show. And the hotel's indoor pool was fantastic. I had trouble getting Tiegan out of it. She won't forget this birthday, that's for sure. Next year, though, don't go quite so overboard."

Considering the jackass of a father she had, his niece deserved to be spoiled every once in a while. Presently he was in a position to do so. "I'm not making any promises."

"You invited Juliette to stay here," Candace said before he could ask any more questions about their time in Boston or start any other conversation.

"She had no power and no wood to start a fire. She had blue lips when I went down to check on her. What was I supposed to do?"

"You could have given her some firewood. It's not like we don't have more than enough."

He'd thrown wood in his truck before driving down with that very intention. It was still in there, in fact. When he saw her, he'd changed his mind. "I thought about it, but I was afraid she'd burn the cottage down."

"Sure, you were." She patted his hand and picked up her tea. "Sometimes, you're a rotten liar. Has anyone ever told you that?"

Not that he recalled, but he didn't make a habit of lying either. Lies tended to make life more complicated than he liked. "I'm not lying. I did bring wood with me when I went down to check on her. It's still in my truck if you don't believe me." He shrugged. "But the next thing I knew, I was inviting her to stay here."

"Must have been those blue eyes of hers." She batted her eyelashes at him and smiled. "I saw the kiss you gave her before she got into her car."

He should have known Candace's what's-going-on antennae would go up the moment he walked outside with Juliette. Honestly, though, his thoughts had been centered on tasting her lips one more time before she left and not who watched them from the window.

"Didn't you tell me at this very table that you didn't want anything to do with her?" Candace asked. "I think you even said something along the lines of if she was a schoolteacher, you'd consider asking her out, but because she comes from a wealthy family, you wanted nothing to do with her."

Yep, he'd said that to her the last time they discussed Juliette, and he didn't need Candace to remind him. "I kissed her. I didn't propose to her."

"You really don't like to admit when you're wrong," she said before sipping her tea.

Did anyone? "Don't you need to get ready for your class tonight?" His sister was enjoying this conversation far too much.

"Nope. So you are going to see her again, right?" Her smile faded a little, a clear sign the conversation was about to take on a more serious tone. "I like her and think she'd be good for you. You need someone in your life besides me, Mom, and Tiegan."

She made it sound like he spent every night at home. True, it'd been months since he'd been on a date, but he met up with his friends on a somewhat regular basis. "You make it sound like I'm a recluse. But since you're so concerned about my life, you'll be glad to know Juliette and I have plans for tomorrow."

Although now that he thought about it, maybe he'd invite her over for dinner tonight. The power had been out for over forty-eight hours. The food in her refrigerator would no longer be any good, and she did need to eat.

His sister's smile returned. "Excellent. What are you doing?"

Good question. "No idea. She asked me, so she's planning the night." And he looked forward to seeing what she came up with.

CHAPTER 11

"THANKS FOR THE INVITE, but I have plans tonight," Aaron said as he logged off his computer and switched off the lights over his desk. After getting ready for his night out, he'd come back in to check his email one last time. He'd been in the middle of answering one when his phone rang.

Like any other Tuesday, he'd spent much of the day in his home office. Today though, he'd struggled to stay focused on his numerous projects because his brain insisted on thinking about Juliette and the time they'd spent alone together as well as last night with Tiegan. Once his sister left for class, he'd called Juliette and invited her to join him and Tiegan for dinner. She'd accepted with no hesitation. He hoped her reason for joining them had more to do with wanting to see him rather than the fact she didn't have much in her kitchen to eat.

Whatever her true reason for coming, he'd been a little jealous of his niece, a fact he wasn't proud of, throughout the evening, because while he'd had Juliette's undivided attention over the weekend, his niece got most of it last night.

While he prepared dinner, Tiegan and Juliette sat at the

kitchen table and discussed their favorite dance styles. Later, while they ate, Juliette listened as Tiegan talked about her past recitals as well as the dance competitions she'd participated in. Naturally, that discussion led to Juliette sharing details about the years she'd spent on stage.

Since he'd had nothing to add—he didn't know the difference between ballet and lyrical—he'd eaten his dinner and watched the interaction between Juliette and his niece. He didn't know if Juliette spent a lot of time around children Tiegan's age, but she was clearly comfortable with his niece. She didn't talk down to her or insist her opinions were wrong. Perhaps even more importantly, Juliette didn't give any sign she'd heard enough from his niece and wanted her to stop talking. While he loved the girl to death, even he sometimes grew tired of listening when she went on and on about a topic. Especially when the topic was one he knew nothing about.

Eventually, Tiegan retreated upstairs to call a friend. With his niece upstairs, though, he figured it was far safer for them to stay in the kitchen. Tiegan had seen people kiss before, and he knew Candace had already had the whole sex talk with her —a conversation he'd been glad she had to handle and not him after Tiegan came home sharing what she'd heard some kids saying on the bus. Still, he didn't want her to come back downstairs and find him with his hand under Juliette's shirt— assuming she let him put it there. Not wanting whatever this thing between them was to move too fast, he'd kept his hands from wandering too far over the weekend.

"You've got plans on a Tuesday night? Doing what?" Junior asked.

He'd known Maxwell Regan, Jr., better known as Junior, since middle school. And it wasn't unheard of for them to meet up with some of their other friends on a random weeknight. If Junior had called last Tuesday and asked him to meet him at Renegade, a pub in Ashford, for a beer and to watch the game, Aaron would have gone.

"I have a date." Juliette hadn't given him any hint as to what they were doing tonight, so even if he wanted to tell Junior more, he couldn't.

"With anyone I know?" Junior might not have lived in Avon his whole life, but he knew many of the residents, especially those that were around their age. "Or is it someone from work?"

The last woman he'd dated had worked at Gilcrest Banking and Financial as his department head's personal assistant. He'd met her one afternoon when he'd gone in to meet with Stephen. If he told Junior he was going out with someone from work now, his friend would believe it without question. But if someone saw him and Juliette together and recognized her, which he suspected some people would, it'd eventually get back to Junior.

"No. Juliette doesn't work at Gilcrest." He saw no reason to give Junior any additional information. Not that he'd want one anyway, but Junior didn't give him a bio sheet on every woman he dated. "Maybe we can get together next week. Say hello to Robby and Broderick for me."

"Will do. And if your date ends early, you know where to find us."

Aaron checked the time before he shoved his cell phone in his back pocket. The doorbell rang before he closed the door.

"I got it." Tiegan flew past him toward the front door. No doubt she'd seen Juliette's car stop out front through the kitchen window and couldn't wait to talk her ear off again.

He followed at a somewhat slower pace, although in truth he wanted to sprint toward the door. Less than twenty-four hours had passed since he last saw Juliette, but damn, he was eager to see her again.

Maybe a little too eager. True, before last weekend, it'd been months since he'd spent time with a woman, but lack of any kind of romantic relationship couldn't account for the overwhelming anticipation that settled in his stomach the moment he stepped out of bed this morning and ruined his concentration all day. No, the blame rested solely on the fact he had a night with Juliette ahead of him.

"Are you staying for dinner again?" his niece asked Juliette as he joined them. "We're having roasted chicken tonight. Nana is already here. She brought over eclairs. She bought them at Sweet Tooth, so they won't be as good as the ones she makes, but they're not bad."

If his mom had brought over eclairs, he hoped his sister saved him one. She knew how much he liked them, regardless of whether they were store-bought or homemade. Although the ones his mom and Candace made were far superior to anything you got from a bakery.

"No, I'm not staying for dinner, but eclairs sound tasty. I'm here to pick up your uncle." Juliette smiled at him, all but knocking him on his ass. Even first thing in the morning when she woke up, the woman was beautiful. When she smiled, though, only one word described her: breathtaking.

Tiegan's expression spoke volumes when she looked over at him. "Oh." She glanced back at their guest. "Are you guys going on a date or something?"

"You don't mind if I borrow your uncle for the night, do you?"

Tiegan shook her head. "Nope. Mom and Nana are always telling Uncle Aaron he needs to go out more. When they find out you're going out, they'll be happy."

Thanks for sharing. Candace needed to remind her daughter that she shouldn't share everything she heard while sitting at the kitchen table. Later, he'd tell his sister that.

"Where are you guys going?" Tiegan asked, oblivious to the fact it wasn't any of her business.

Juliette pressed her lips together as if trying not to either smile or laugh and looked at him briefly before turning her attention back to Tiegan. Finally, she cleared her throat. "Just to dinner and stuff. Nothing super exciting."

"You guys should go to Adventure Park. I went to a birthday party there for my friend Jasmine. They have indoor skydiving and surfing in a gigantic wave pool. It's so much fun. I don't remember where it was, but I can ask Mom. She drove me there."

While indoor skydiving or even surfing might be a blast, it didn't strike him as a great place for a first date. And although they'd spent considerable time together, tonight was their first date.

"It sounds like a great place, and I love surfing. Maybe your uncle and I can go some other time."

"You know how to surf?" Tiegan's eyes grew wide, and her voice went up a notch. "I *so* want to try it. It looked like so much fun."

Juliette nodded. "I think you'd love it. If it's okay with your mom, the two of us can go to Adventure Park and do it together."

For the umpteenth time since Saturday, his conscience took the opportunity to point out he'd unfairly judged Juliette before getting to know her.

"Mom, did you hear Juliette?" Tiegan asked when she spotted Candace headed toward them. "Can she take me?"

"I did. And we'll discuss it later. For now, I need you to set the table for dinner. And don't forget napkins this time." She walked past him and hugged Juliette. He'd never under-stood why so many women insisted on greeting each other that way. "Thank you for taking my brother off my hands tonight, Juliette. I owe you one."

The laugh she'd been holding in during her conversation with Tiegan escaped. "Consider it repayment for the baking lessons. Does he have a curfew I need to keep in mind?"

Candace seemed to consider the question before she answered. "No, but he has to work tomorrow, so don't keep him out too late. And if he doesn't behave himself, let me know."

"I'll try to get him home before midnight," Juliette promised, taking his hand and opening the door at the same time. Juliette led him outside, but once the door stood between them and the house's occupants, she turned to face. "I missed you today." An easy smile played at the corners of her mouth as she put her arms over his shoulders.

Her breasts brushed against his chest first, and all the blood in his body started its descent south. Before he could do one of the many things he'd been thinking about all day, she pressed a featherlight kiss against his mouth. As they stood there, he wondered how she'd react if he suggested they spend the next several hours at her cottage instead of doing whatever she had planned.

Pulling her lips away, she allowed her hands to slowly slip from his shoulders and across his chest before falling back to her sides. "We should go."

Somehow his brain strung some words together. Exactly how, he had no idea. "Do you want me to drive tonight?" He knew the area, she didn't, and regardless of where she intended to take him, he could get there without the use of GPS.

"Nope. I've got it."

He'd hoped she'd hand over her car keys and ask him to drive. Even as a kid, he'd had a thing for cars, and he'd love a chance to drive Juliette's Porsche. But he didn't argue as he followed her to the plum-colored vehicle. He'd never seen a Porsche or any other car painted that color. If her car had a custom paint job, he wondered what other extras it might have under the hood.

JULIETTE LOOKED at the shoes on the counter. She'd worn some ugly footwear on various photoshoots, but the footwear the bowling alley employee had just set down elevated the word to a whole new level. Whoever had designed them needed to have their eyesight checked.

Aaron accepted his pair of shoes with no hesitation and thanked the employee. "Something wrong?"

Yep, I'm wondering if we should have gone someplace else.

Like she'd planned, they'd eaten dinner at the Stomping Ground, a restaurant in Ashford right on the lake. If anyone recognized her, they left her alone and went about their business. Aaron hadn't been so lucky. First, their waitress, a woman who looked old enough to be Juliette's mom, recognized Aaron and spent time inquiring about how he'd been, as well as his sisters. Once she left, he'd shared the woman had been his and Candace's eighth grade math teacher and that he'd heard she worked at the restaurant to keep herself busy since retiring. Later, while they'd been enjoying dessert, his friend Hunter and his wife sat down at the table next to them. It hadn't escaped her that when Aaron made introductions, he didn't mention her last name, where she was from, or how they'd met.

"Nope." She picked up her shoes and promised her feet a pedicure soon to make up for forcing them to wear footwear that was sure to be as uncomfortable as it was ugly.

Although a Tuesday night, many of the lanes were already being used, and they walked toward the far end of the building. "The last time I bowled, I was with my nephew, Mason.

That had to be more than a year ago, but I think we spent more time in the arcade that day than we did out here bowling," Aaron said.

They'd passed the noisy arcade when they'd walked inside. She'd never been big into video games, but for someone who enjoyed them, the room they'd passed would be like heaven.

"This is my first time."

Aaron stopped at an empty lane. "You've *never* been bowling?"

Shaking her head, she sat down so she could change her shoes.

"Let me get this right. You've been surfing but not bowling?" Sitting down next to her, Aaron untied his shoes.

"I love the water, and my family used to vacation a lot in Hawaii. As far as I know, no one in my family bowls. I don't think any of my friends do either."

"Maybe we better not keep score tonight."

She'd never played, but how hard could it be? You rolled a ball down the floor toward some pins and knocked them down. "Whatever you want. It doesn't matter to me."

Juliette quickly learned how wrong she'd been. Bowling might look easy, but there was a lot more to it than simply rolling a ball.

After managing yet another gutter ball, she turned and walked back to where Aaron sat nursing his beer. "Maybe I should've taken Tiegan's suggestion and brought you to the indoor skydiving place instead." Dropping into the stiff plastic seat next to him, she narrowed her eyes at him. "What's so funny?" Aaron found something amusing. She hoped it wasn't her debut performance bowling tonight.

"I was just thinking about something that happened when I went bowling with some friends in college." Without continuing, he stood and started toward the ball return.

Clearly, the memory included a humorous story; otherwise Aaron wouldn't have a grin stretching across his face. She liked a good laugh as much as the next person. "Aren't you going to share?"

Rather than retrieve his ball and take his turn, Aaron came back and sat down. "There was a bowling alley not far from campus. Every Thursday night was college night, so it was half price to play. Maybe once a month a bunch of us would go over and play. Anyway, a guy named Jim came with us one night. I don't even remember his last name. I didn't know him well. He played on the football team with my roommate, Lee. He was a nice guy, but he was the walking embodiment of the dumb jock stereotype. I don't know how he ever got into college, never mind how he graduated."

"I knew some people in college like that."

Of course, she also knew how they'd gotten in, and it'd been because of who they were related to. Rather than share that tidbit of information, she picked up her beer and took a sip while waiting for Aaron to continue. She wasn't much of a beer drinker; instead, she preferred fruity cocktails with little umbrellas in them or wine, especially French wine. But the lounge at the bowling alley had several beers on tap from local New Hampshire breweries, and when the bartender asked what she wanted, she'd ordered the same as Aaron rather than inquire about the selection of wines available. As far as beers went, what she had was the tastiest she'd ever tried.

Aaron took a gulp from his glass before he continued. "Like you, Jim had never bowled before, and he had a few beers before we even got there. After his second or third turn, Jim left to use the restroom, and my roommate decided to switch Jim's bowling ball with a different one. When he returned and tried to use it, his fingers wouldn't fit in the holes. Lee told him that sometimes the first time you bowled your fingers swelled up because they weren't used to it. Lee suggested he go run them under cold water so the swelling would go down. While Jim was doing that, Lee switched the bowling balls again, so he had the one he started the night using. Of course, his fingers fit on his next turn. Lee did that to him two or three more times."

"He never caught on?" She could imagine someone falling for the trick once, but multiple times? It seemed like a person would at least get suspicious and wonder if something odd was going on.

"Nope. He just kept going back to the restroom and running his hands under cold water each time. Maybe if he hadn't been drinking, he would've figured it out. I don't know."

"Did anyone ever tell him what happened that night?"

Shaking his head, he lifted the glass toward his mouth again. "Not that I know of."

"So you're telling me either I shouldn't use the ladies' room while we're here or if I do, I need to bring my bowling ball with me."

Aaron set his glass down and moved closer, his knees bumping against her leg as heat replaced the humor in his eyes. "You're safe from practical jokes with me." He brushed his fingers across her cheek before cupping the back of her head. "I'd rather spend our time together doing things we'll both enjoy." His lips touched hers. The feel of them moving back and forth across hers blocked out the sounds and smells around her—a remarkable feat, considering where they were.

Unlike when they kissed outside his house, Aaron pulled back first. "We should finish our game."

She agreed. While she was having fun despite the uncomfortable footwear, she'd like to spend some time alone away from prying eyes before they parted for the night. "It's your turn."

He traced his fingertips along her jaw one last time before standing and walking to the ball return, and her eyes followed him every step of the way. He moved with a nonchalant grace. And his jeans and sweater accentuated rather than hid the muscled body they covered.

Far too preoccupied with staring at Aaron and his jean-covered butt, she didn't notice the two women approaching until one of them spoke.

"Excuse me," a female voice said.

Juliette pulled her eyes away from the pleasant view and found two women around her age standing near the seat Aaron vacated.

"Did you graduate from Ashford High School?" one of the women asked.

"Sorry, no, I didn't."

"I told you she didn't go to school with us, Noella," the woman's companion said. "But you do look really familiar. Do you belong to the Ashford Athletic Club? We both go there."

If she told them her name, they'd figure out quickly why she looked familiar. She didn't intend to do that. At the same time, if they came right out and asked if she were Juliette Belmont, she wouldn't lie either.

"No, I don't go to that gym. I'm new to the area."

Done with his turn, Aaron sat down next to her. "Hi, Sandy," he said. "How have you been?"

"Not too bad. Do you remember my cousin Noella?" She nodded toward the woman who'd first spoken when they approached Juliette.

With a nod, he rested his arm on the back of her seat. "It's nice to see you again," he said before looking in Juliette's direction. "Sandy used to teach at Dance Dynamics with Candace. Now they do classes through the parks and rec department together."

This was Candace's friend Sandy. The one who used to teach acro. She'd heard a lot about her from Tiegan. If she went ahead with her plan to open a dance studio in town, Sandy might be someone she'd want teaching there. She already planned to ask Candace to join her, but the two of them couldn't teach all the classes.

"Sandy, Noella, this is my—" Aaron paused for a split second before he finished his sentence. "—friend Juliette."

Evidently, he didn't know where they stood either. Before the evening ended, she'd wanted that cleared up between them.

Juliette held her breath while Sandy's eyes searched her face as if suddenly the answer to why she looked familiar would appear written on her skin. "I know I've seen you somewhere, Juliette. I just can't put my finger on where." Finally, she nudged her companion with her elbow. "We should go, Noella. Dennis and Vince are probably wondering what happened to us. I'll see you later, Aaron. Juliette, it was nice meeting you."

She watched the two women walk away. "I can't take you anywhere without running into people who know you," she said teasingly.

"Hey, they came over here because you looked familiar, not to say hello to me."

"I'm not sure that's the only reason they came over. Sandy couldn't take her eyes off you once you sat down." She didn't know if Sandy was married or not, but she had a thing for Aaron.

"Candace and Sandy have known each other since they were about Tiegan's age. They both danced at Dance Dynamics long before they worked there. And more than once, Candace has attempted to set us up."

She'd fixed her cousin Alec up with Holly, and they'd gone out and had some fun together, but she'd never tried to get her brother together with one of her friends. While she adored her friends, she'd always known they were all wrong for Scott.

"But I made the mistake of going out with one of my sister's friends when we were in high school. Even if Sandy was my type, which she isn't, I wouldn't get involved with her, because she and Candace are so close."

She respected his decision. Not that her brother knew it, but one of his friends had approached her last year. Although she liked him as a person and found him handsome, she'd turned him down rather than risk hurting her brother's friendship.

"She might call my sister later and ask about you. If she does, Candace will tell her you're a guest at the campground. You don't have anything to worry about."

She hadn't known the Wrights long, but she trusted them. "I'm not worried. And if Sandy realizes why I look familiar, oh well. There's not much I can do about it."

They hadn't been keeping score, but they had been keeping track of how many frames they played, and they were about to start their tenth. "If we leave after this frame, you can come down to the cottage and have a drink or two and still be home by midnight." After venturing into Gorham's Shop and Save earlier in the day to restock her kitchen, she'd popped into the liquor store next door and purchased a few bottles of both red and white wine.

"I'll do whatever you want tonight."

CHAPTER 12

AARON FOLLOWED Juliette into the cottage and immediately noticed the bright orange sacks of firewood near the woodstove. Either she'd gone to the supermarket today, or Mrs. Lambert had made another delivery because Gorham's Shop and Save was the only place in town that sold those cords of wood. And usually, only tourists bought them, because per piece it was far more expensive than what Valley Landscaping sold.

"I don't think you need to worry about another power outage." He gestured toward the wood while removing his jacket and putting it on the back of a chair. "What happened over the weekend isn't common."

She hung her jacket on a kitchen chair before getting two wineglasses from a cabinet—glasses she must have either purchased or brought with her because while the kitchen came equipped with a lot of items, wineglasses were not among them. "I want to be prepared just in case. And if I don't use it in here, I thought we could use it in the firepit outside. We could roast marshmallows and make s'mores. I don't even remember the last time I did that."

She'd said we *could use it, not* I *can use it.* Aaron liked the sound of that. He also liked the fact he'd at least popped into her thoughts today. Especially since thoughts of her had distracted him so much.

"I was going to open the merlot, but if you'd rather, I have a bottle of pinot grigio."

When it came to red wine, he'd never been a fan of merlot. He much preferred zinfandel. "I'm more in the mood for white wine, but if you want merlot, I'll drink it."

Juliette returned the red wine glasses to the cabinet and took out some intended for white wine. At least when it came to wine, no one would say she wasn't prepared. "Nope. I'm happy with the pinot."

He watched her leave the glasses on the counter and move to the refrigerator. Although perhaps move didn't do justice to her body in motion. Every one of her movements had a graceful element to it, making her a walking piece of art. Even if she hadn't told him she'd danced most of her life, he would've guessed it.

"Do you want a snack? I picked up all kinds of fruit today and some cheeses." She filled the two glasses as she spoke. Even while she did that, she'd had an elegance about her he'd never seen before.

He'd been hungry for the past forty minutes. If he'd been at home, he would have either raided the refrigerator for any leftovers or rummaged through the cabinets for something quick and easy. "Only if you're having something."

Rather than join him, she set about preparing them a snack. "Sometime soon, we should check out the indoor skydiving place Tiegan mentioned. It sounds like an interesting place."

He'd learned to scuba dive, although he only managed to do it once or twice a year, and he often went mountain climbing. But he'd never tried skydiving. Even when his buddy

Robby tried it a few years ago and invited him along, he'd passed. No doubt, indoor skydiving was worlds apart from the jumping out of an airplane type. "I'm willing to give it a try. Tiegan didn't stop talking about it after she went to the party there."

"Tiegan kept talking? I don't believe it." Pressing a hand against her chest, she feigned a shocked expression.

"I know it's hard to believe. The girl barely speaks."

"If you ask my mom, she'd say I was a lot like Tiegan at her age." She set a tray down on the small coffee table and handed him a wineglass before picking up the second and sitting down.

"She's probably going to ask you about going surfing there. You don't have to take her." Juliette carrying on a conversation with his niece while they ate dinner was one thing, but an all-day outing was another.

"As long as it's okay with your sister, I'd love to take her. I think it'll be fun. Or we can take her together. Maybe we could try both the surfing and the skydiving while we're there."

The three of them going sounded like an excellent idea. Not that he didn't trust Juliette alone with his niece, but in case of an emergency, he'd rather Tiegan have either her mom, nana, or him close by. And while emergencies probably didn't occur often, they could happen. "I'll check out Adventure Park's website tomorrow."

"Speaking of tomorrow, I'm meeting Caryn Ferguson around three to look at some homes and the old dance studio. If you're not busy, I'd like you to come with me and give me a second opinion."

If he showed up with her, not only would half the town know Juliette Belmont had rented a cottage at the campground by dinnertime, but they'd also be on their way to the altar thanks to Caryn. He'd never cared about rumors before, and he didn't care now. But Juliette deserved a heads-up.

"Caryn knows a lot of people, and she's got a big mouth. If I come with you, everyone's going to think we're together. It wouldn't surprise me if people start saying we're engaged. Rumors have a way of taking on a life of their own in town."

She reached for a strawberry but, at the last minute, snagged a square of cheese off the plate instead. "Are you married?" she asked before popping the cheese in her mouth and leaving him scratching his head.

"What?"

"I asked if you are married."

Well, at least he didn't have a problem with his hearing. "No, of course not. What does that have to do with anything?"

"I don't care if people know we're together. But you sound worried, so I wanted to make sure you weren't hiding a wife up in your attic or something. Been there, done that, and I have no desire to repeat the experience." She smiled and patted his cheek before getting another piece of cheese.

"It doesn't bother me if people know we're seeing each other. But I thought you wanted to keep as low a profile as possible while you're here."

While she considered his words, he drank his wine. He didn't know what type she'd purchased, but he tasted a hint of nectarine, not something he associated with any kind of wine.

"When I first checked in, I did, but the media is already on the hunt for a juicy new story or a celebrity wedding. Yesterday there was only a brief mention of me on the *Star Insider* and *Today Magazine's* websites. I didn't find anything anywhere else."

She'd admitted her primary reason for coming to Avon had been to escape the spotlight. If the media no longer considered her headline material and she decided against purchasing a home here, how much longer would it be before she packed up and headed back to New York City? A scenario he found far more likely than her moving to Avon and opening a business.

"Hey, I don't care what Caryn tells people. If you want me to tag along tomorrow and give you my opinion, I will. Where are the houses you're looking at?" Whether she moved there permanently or left next month, he'd focus on enjoying their time together and not what might happen.

"NOT EVEN ELEVEN O'CLOCK, and you're home," Candace greeted when he walked into the living room. "Either Juliette wanted to make sure you didn't fall asleep while you sat at your computer, or your date didn't go as well I hoped."

"Were you waiting up for me?"

"Not really. I started this new series last week and turned on the next episode after Tiegan went to bed. One turned into another and another," she said, reaching for the remote and switching off the television.

He'd had the same thing happen to him. But he wouldn't put it past Candace to have turned the series on knowing it would help her stay awake until he came home.

Although past the time he normally went to bed, if he went up now, he'd stare at the ceiling. A better use of his time would be to sit down and answer whatever questions his sister tossed at him. And if he didn't answer them tonight, she'd simply ask him tomorrow.

"I heard you went bowling." She made her statement before his butt even touched the seat of the armchair. "Sandy called me."

Wow, what a shocker. "Before or after she left Silver Lanes?"

"Probably after. Sandy asked about Juliette, insisting she'd seen her somewhere, and she wanted to know how serious things were between the two of you. Sandy wouldn't have asked about the status of your relationship with Vince around, and I know she was seeing him tonight."

"What did you tell her?"

"The truth. I told her Juliette was renting a cottage here, and I had no idea where things stood between the two of you."

He'd known Candace wouldn't tell Sandy where she'd seen Juliette's face. More than likely, Sandy would figure it out at some point. She wasn't stupid.

"What else did you do besides go bowling?"

"Dinner at the Stomping Ground before, and afterward, we went back to the cottage for some wine."

"Only wine?"

"Well, we had some fruit and cheese with the wine." Just because they were both adults didn't mean he couldn't enjoy giving his baby sister a hard time.

Candace threw him a dirty look. "That's not what I meant, and you know it."

She never asked about his sex life, and he never brought it up. But he'd answer her questions tonight because he had nothing to hide. "We talked and had some wine. Then she gave me a ride back up." He told her he could use the flashlight on his cell phone and walk, but she'd insisted.

Candace made a noise in the back of her throat and pulled her feet up on the sofa. "I'm a little surprised."

Did she think he slept with every woman he went out with? He hoped she knew him better than that. "Why?"

She shrugged. "Just am. But I'm the one asking the questions, remember?"

How could he forget?

"Did you have fun?"

The most fun he'd had in a long time. "Yeah, and we have plans for tomorrow."

"That's awesome. If Sandy asks again, I'll have to tell her things are getting serious."

After their house-hunting expedition, Sandy might hear they were engaged, thanks to the rumor mill.

"What's on tomorrow's agenda?"

"Caryn Ferguson is showing her homes and the old dance studio. Juliette asked me to come along."

"*Caryn's* taking her around, and you're going too? I won't need to call Sandy and give her an update on your relationship," she said with a laugh. "The looking at houses thing is self-explanatory, but why is she looking at the dance studio?"

What did they say about assuming things? Considering the time they'd spent together and their mutual love of dance, it had seemed natural Juliette would have shared her idea with his sister. Now that he'd let the cat out of the bag, he'd share what he knew and apologize to Juliette in case she hadn't mentioned it to his sister for a reason.

"She's not only thinking about moving to the area, but she's considering opening a dance studio in Avon. I don't know any of the specifics. You'll have to ask her."

"Next time I see her, I will. Right now, I'm heading up to bed. I'm subbing at the elementary school tomorrow." Standing, Candace folded the throw blanket she'd been using and set it down on the sofa. "I'm glad you got your head out of your butt and went out with Juliette tonight. I knew you two would have fun together."

They'd already discussed how he'd been wrong. He didn't need his sister to bring it up again. "See you in the morning. Have a good night's sleep." He didn't see himself getting one. Nope, he expected he'd be replaying his evening and wondering what tomorrow would bring.

∾

WIDE AWAKE DESPITE THE TIME, Juliette pulled out her cell phone as she headed upstairs to her bedroom.

I know you're dying for the details. Call if you want to talk.

After sending the text message off to Holly, she grabbed a clean pair of pajamas. Her nosy friend expected a full report about their night. Since she knew darn well she wouldn't fall asleep if she got into bed, she needed a way to pass the time. A chat with Holly would satisfy that and her friend's curiosity.

Her cell phone rang before she added her jeans to the laundry hamper.

"I've been thinking about you all night," Holly said in lieu of a proper greeting. "Isn't it a little early to be home already?"

If they'd been in the city, perhaps their evening would've lasted longer. Instead of going back to her place after bowling, or whatever other activity they did after dinner, maybe they would've gone to one of her favorite clubs and spent time there before going back to her condo for drinks. Then again, perhaps not. She honestly couldn't picture Aaron at any of the clubs she liked to visit.

"Holly, did you forget where I am?"

"True. At this time, only the movie theater is open, and even that will be closing soon. Did you have fun?"

How should she answer Holly? The evening had been like no other date she'd ever gone on. At the same time, it'd been one of the best nights out she'd had in a long time, and not because she'd suddenly discovered how much she loved bowling. The evening's enjoyment rested on Aaron's shoulders.

"Delightful." She couldn't recall ever using the word to describe a date, but it fit.

"You found bowling delightful? Maybe you've been in Avon too long. I think you should consider coming back to the city this week and spending a few days here."

Driving back to New York City was the last thing she planned to do this week. "Knock it off. You love it here."

"In small doses. We can talk about that later. First, tell me what else you did besides bowl, and then I want to know what made your night with Aaron 'delightful.'"

She pictured Holly making air quotes. "We went for dinner at the restaurant you suggested. I found it a little odd that a retired teacher Aaron had in middle school waited on us. But he didn't."

"It's not unusual for teachers in town to retire and work a part-time job afterward to keep busy. Actually, a lot of them work as substitutes for the district. Do you remember who waited on you?"

"A Mrs. Fuller. Aaron said he had her for eighth-grade math."

"I had her for math too. I can't believe she retired. She was ridiculously tough but a great teacher. Sorry, I didn't mean to get off topic. You had dinner followed by bowling. Anything else?"

"After we left Silver Lanes, we went back to my cottage, had some wine, and talked."

"Did anyone recognize you while you were out?" Holly asked.

When Holly had called her earlier in the day, they'd discussed the possibility that someone in town would recognize her and the likelihood everyone in town would soon after know she was staying at the campground.

"Two women at the bowling alley asked if I graduated high school with them because I looked familiar, but otherwise, no one said anything to me." No one had approached her while she shopped either.

"I'm sure you're happy about that." Holly didn't give her a chance to reply. "Dinner, bowling, and talking sounds like a rather standard date for anyone living in Avon. What made it 'delightful'?"

"Aaron. He's not like anyone I've been out with before. He's easy to talk to—"

"And easy on the eyes," Holly added.

"Well yeah, but so was Daniel." Although if she ranked the two men according to their looks, she'd give Aaron a perfect ten and Daniel a seven. Before the disaster involving his wife, she would have given the man an eight and a half, but somehow knowing what a creep he was diminished his looks.

"True enough. Please continue. I promise not to interrupt again."

I'll believe that when it happens. "He doesn't treat me like an empty-headed idiot." Way too many times, she'd gone out with a man who assumed her career choice of modeling somehow meant she couldn't even handle simple addition. "And he listens to me."

"You mean he doesn't just stare at your boobs while you're talking and then not realize when you've stopped? I didn't think men like that existed." Holly's laughter traveled through the phone, and Juliette smiled.

"Hard to believe, but yes. Maybe they only exist in New Hampshire, and that's why they're so difficult to track down." Flopping back on the bed, she stared at the ceiling fan. "There's something else about him. I don't know what, but I enjoy being around him. You know how I felt unsatisfied with life?" Other than Aaron, Holly was the only person she'd shared those sentiments and her desire to make some changes with.

"Yeah."

"Well, I don't feel that way anymore. I didn't expect it, but I'm happier here in general, and even more so when I'm around Aaron."

She hadn't seen a single house or stepped inside the dance studio, but her gut told her tomorrow she'd be making an offer on at least the studio. Since they'd discussed her state of mind before she left New York, now seemed like a good time to drop the news on Holly.

"I'm thinking about opening a dance studio."

"Huh, sounds like it could be fun, and your name alone will give it a boost over most of the other ones around. Whereabouts in the city are you thinking? And have you told Pierre?"

Yeah, she still needed to have that conversation. "Not yet. I'm waiting until it's a done deal. But if I do, the studio won't be in Manhattan. It'll be here. The school in town closed last June, and the building is for sale. I'm going to look at it and some houses in both Avon and Ashford tomorrow." The more people she told about her plans, the louder her conscience insisted it was the right move.

Dead silence followed her statement. She'd have to mark it down on her calendar as the first time Holly Lambert had no response.

"Holly," she said after a few seconds. "Are you still there? Should I call my brother and ask him to come and check on you?"

"Funny. I'm trying to wrap my head around things."

Juliette pictured Holly's eyebrows scrunched together as her friend digested the bombshell she'd dropped.

"You… you're considering moving to Avon and opening

a dance school? I know you wanted a change and were tired of the photoshoots, but isn't this a little… uh, drastic?"

"Maybe, but I've got a good feeling about it."

"I'd need more than a good feeling before I gave up my career and left Manhattan to live in Avon again. But hey, to each their own. Whatever you decide, I'll support you."

She'd known Holly would support her decision, but it was still nice to hear.

"If you want to reschedule to Thursday, I can drive up tomorrow and go with you," Holly offered. "A second opinion can be useful."

In the past, she'd consulted Holly for advice, and she appreciated her offer to come and help her now. But it wasn't Holly's opinion she wanted this time. "Thanks for offering, but Aaron's coming with me tomorrow."

"I can't say I blame you for picking him over me," Holly teased. "Let me know if you make an offer on anything. Sometime next week, I might come up and visit. I can look at houses with you then, if you're still looking and Aaron's not available."

"I'll keep you up to date." Juliette stifled a yawn. She'd been wide awake when she answered the phone. Now she wanted to crawl between the sheets and go to sleep. Thankfully, she didn't have far to go to make that happen. "I'm going to bed, Holly. I'll talk to you later."

Moments after her head hit the pillow, she fell asleep, and once again, Aaron invaded her dreams.

CHAPTER 13

THE BRIGHT PINK awning caught Juliette's eye even before she turned into the parking lot. It, along with the equally bright pink door, called a person's attention to the white building better than a neon sign. If she purchased the place, both would have to go.

She put her car in Park and turned off the ignition. For the moment, they were the only ones in the parking lot, but they had arrived ten minutes early. "I wonder if the pink theme continues inside?"

"I don't think I have ever been in the building. Not a fan of pink?" Aaron asked as he unbuckled his seat belt.

Juliette followed his lead, but her eyes never left the former dance studio. The pink color aside, from here the structure looked well-maintained. It was a promising sign.

"It's okay, but not my favorite."

"Neither of my sisters like pink either. And Tiegan's favorite color, at least right now, is dark green. Speaking of my sister, I told her you're thinking about opening a dance school in town. I assumed you'd already told her. I'm sorry."

By the tone of his voice, she'd have thought he shared her

deepest secret with Candace. "Until I talked to Holly yester-day, you were the only person I told. But don't worry about it. It's not a big deal. And if I go ahead with this, I'm going to ask Candace if she'd like to teach a few classes. I was also going to ask her if Sandy might like to teach since they worked together before, and both do the classes through the park and rec department."

"You'll probably get a yes to both questions. If Candace could have afforded to purchase the school when Merry retired, she would've. I'd say the same was true in Sandy's case," Aaron explained before gesturing toward the driver-side window. "Caryn's here."

Excitement zigzagged through her body as she stepped out of the car and waited with Aaron for the real estate agent to join them. When Caryn finally exited the metallic gray Miata, she had two folders in one hand and a leather purse large enough to carry a small child in over her shoul-der. Juliette couldn't even begin to imagine what the woman brought around with her that required her to use such a bag.

"I hope you haven't been waiting long. A last-minute call came in about a closing next week, and I had to deal with it before I left the office," Caryn greeted, approaching them.

"We just got here ourselves," Juliette assured the woman.

"Good. I hate to keep people waiting. When you called, I thought your name sounded familiar. Now I know why."

Did she have her recent magazine appearances and asso-ciation with Daniel to thank for Caryn recognizing her or was the woman referring to all the times she'd appeared in the fragrance section at Caryn's favorite department store on a poster advertising a new scent from one of the many compa-nies she'd modeled for? She'd prefer the latter but wasn't going to hold her breath.

"It's so nice to meet you." The older woman's attention

moved to Aaron. "I don't remember the last time I saw you, Aaron. How have you been?"

"Fine, and you?" Aaron replied, although Juliette doubted the woman was paying attention to anything he said. In fact, Juliette could all but see the wheels spinning in Caryn's head as she took in Aaron's arm across her shoulders and tried to determine the exact nature of their relationship.

"Busy but well," the other woman finally answered, proving she'd been listening while determining what to tell everyone she knew. "I put all the information about each of the properties we're looking at today in here as well as some information about the Ferguson Real Estate Agency." She handed over one of the two folders before using the key in the lockbox to open the studio door.

Someone liked the color pink. Juliette stepped into a small waiting area. Although a light gray carpet covered the floor, the owner had painted the walls the same shade of pink as the main door. Without even taking another step, she could see the color continued on into the office located off to the left.

"The building is forty-six years old. Originally it was an apartment complex. Merry Baxter, the current owner, purchased it thirty-five years ago and remodeled the entire place. We've been friends for a long time, and I remember when she first bought the building. She spent hours with the contractors, making sure everything was laid out to fit her vision."

From the outside, Juliette never would have guessed the building was almost fifty years old.

"On this level, there is the office, two restrooms, and three dance studios. There are two more upstairs," Caryn continued as she flipped to another page in her folder. "Four years ago, Merry redid the wood floors in all the studios. The paperwork says the wood is beech. She also replaced the HVAC system seven years ago."

Yep, so far, it sounded like Merry Baxter had kept the interior as well maintained as the exterior.

"Like the rest of the town, the building has its own septic. However, it does have town water. You might already know this, but most of the town relies on well water."

Oh, she knew that and what it meant when you lost power. If she bought a home in town, the first thing she'd do was have a generator installed.

Taking Aaron's hand, Juliette followed Caryn down a short hallway and into a much larger waiting area. Pastel pink covered the walls in this area, although the white cubbies and hooks lining the longest one helped break up the color scheme.

Opening the door closest to her, she stepped inside and switched on the lights. An immaculate floor gleamed despite the building having been closed up for so long, and mirrors covered one entire wall. Of course, the other three walls reminded her of bubble gum, but a fresh coat of paint would take care of that problem.

"This is the largest of the three rooms on this floor," Caryn said from the doorway. "Studio One is the smallest." She gestured across the waiting room to a white door with the words Studio One stenciled in hot pink on it.

She expected the other two rooms to be both well cared for and painted some shade of pink. She ended up being right on both accounts.

"I think Mrs. Baxter had an unhealthy obsession with the color pink," Aaron whispered in her ear as they followed Caryn up to the second level.

"Really? I'm not getting that impression."

Aaron squeezed her hand and smiled. "As far as I can see, the only problem with the building seems to be the color scheme. Painting isn't hard."

She agreed. The color aside, she liked the layout of the

building, and even the smallest of studios provided sufficient space for a small class to practice without getting in each other's way. And since the major items like floors and the heating system were all new, she wouldn't need to replace them. At least not anytime soon.

The stairs opened into an extra-wide hallway. Cubbies similar to those downstairs filled the farthermost wall. Along with the storage space, the current owner had added a restroom to this floor, so dancers wouldn't need to use the ones downstairs.

Juliette opened the door marked Studio Four and flipped on the lights. Three magenta-painted walls greeted her while mirrors covered the fourth. Well, at least the owner was consistent. She could have painted each part of the building a different color of the rainbow.

"The sale of the property includes the mats," Caryn said, pointing toward the blue carpet bonded foam rolls left by the mirror. "I have no idea what they are used for, but I'm sure you do."

"You would use them if you're teaching an acro dance class." She'd seen acro dance routines, but she'd never taken a class. According to Tiegan, though, Sandy had taught it before, so maybe she would be willing to do it again. "It incorporates a lot of gymnastics moves; that's why the mats are used."

"Never heard of it. It must be something they started teaching here after my daughter stopped coming. Feel free to walk around. Once you're all set here, we can head over to Oak Ridge Lane."

WHEN THEY WALKED out of the dance studio, Juliette dropped her car keys in his hand and asked him to drive so she could read through the paperwork Caryn gave her. He'd agreed happily. More than once on the ride over to Oak Ridge Lane, he had to remind himself to slow down. How Juliette managed to drive the car and not get a speeding ticket every other day was a miracle. Then again, maybe she got pulled over all the time, and the moment the police officers saw her face, they forgot why they'd pulled her over. Whatever the case, if they weren't so expensive, he'd have a Porsche instead of a Ford parked in his garage.

For at least the fifth time, Aaron reduced his speed and then turned onto Timberlane Road, which would eventually bring him to Oak Ridge. Located along the westernmost portion of the lake, he hardly every drove to this part of town. Other than a handful of homes and Camp Evergreen, a kids' summer camp, there wasn't anything out this way. And unless they'd done construction recently, Timberlane and Oak Ridge were the only paved streets on this side of the lake. There was, or at least there had been, a dirt road leading to an old log cabin, but who knew if either remained.

"The address we're going to is number twelve," Juliette said, speaking for the first time since they'd left the dance studio.

He would've been able to figure out which house they were headed to without the additional information. At one time, a number of small houses, several of which had only been used as vacation homes in the summer, lined Oak Ridge. Now only three remained: a mini-mansion and two small cottages that had belonged to the same family for four generations. The cottages were so old they had outside showers, or at least they had when he'd visited his friend Bill there as a kid, and no central heat. And if it'd been up to the owners of Twelve Oak Ridge Lane, the cottages wouldn't be on the dead-end street either.

"I'm surprised the owners are selling this already. They

only built the house about four years ago." He didn't know how long it had taken to complete or when the owners moved in, but he remembered when his dad refused to sell land to the couple. Roughly a year later, they started construction here instead.

Juliette closed the folder and tucked it on the floor next to her purse. "If I buy this house, I won't have to worry about any noisy neighbors keeping me up at night."

"Yeah, no one will be stopping by and asking to borrow flour either."

"Are there even any other homes on this street?"

Turning onto the driveway, he wondered what the multi-millionaires who'd first approached his dad had finally constructed. With it set so far back from the road, curious eyes could only view the home from the water or by driving down the driveway.

"There used to be more. The owners of this place made generous offers to all the other property owners. Only one family turned them down. They own the two cottages at the end of the road. Once the couple owned the properties, they tore down the five or six buildings that were here. They also purchased some land from Camp Evergreen, the kids' summer camp we passed."

"Sounds drastic and unnecessarily expensive. They couldn't find any other land in town?"

A large Victorian-style house complete with a tower came into view, looking about as different from what he'd expected as possible. "There isn't a lot of land available on the lake. And the few lots that come up from time to time are usually small. The people who built this first tried to get my dad to sell them some land. He refused all their offers. I'm not sure I would've said no to their final one, but it wasn't up to me."

Since they'd built the house in a style popular over a century ago, he expected the interior to also replicate a home from the same period. He'd never been more wrong. While the main foyer fell in line with what he expected, the kitchen resembled something from a sci-fi movie, while the largest of the two living rooms on the first floor had a whole safari theme going on complete with an animal skin rug. And forget about the music room. It appeared as though someone had plucked it straight out of one of those Gilded-Age mansions built in Newport during the late 1800s. He'd never meet the owners, but either they were the most eccentric couple on the planet, allowed a five-year-old to do the decorating, or simply had no taste.

"I remember when they built this house, Caryn. The owners went through a lot of effort to get a spot on the lake. Do you know why they are selling?" It wouldn't surprise him if the owners had woken up one morning, noticed what a disastrous mess they'd created, and decided it was easier to sell and start over than to redo what they had.

"Deidra decided she wanted something in the mountains instead. Personally, I'd rather be on the lake, but to each their own. They started construction on a log cabin in Franconia late last summer."

He loved the mountains, but if given a choice between seeing the lake every morning or the mountains, he'd take the water.

"Deidra and Mateo are motivated to sell, and the price includes all the furnishings. I'm sure you noticed the property has been on the market since September." Caryn led them down to a set of french doors, and he wondered what decorating faux pas waited for them on the other side.

Rather than find a home office decorated as if it belonged in the medieval period or a game room that resembled an old 1920s speakeasy, two things he wouldn't have been surprised about at this point, he walked into an indoor pool area more or less devoid of any decoration except for the lounge chairs and a hot tub in the far corner.

"Between the three of us, the unique décor has turned off the few potential buyers I've brought through."

Unique décor. Was that what you called it? "I wonder why?" he whispered into Juliette's ear when she paused to open the sauna door and peek inside.

"I've known Deidra for several years. She likes extremes. I recommended they make some changes before putting the home on the market, but she didn't see the need. Nina, their listing agent, should have told them the same thing."

There was no For Sale sign out front, but he'd assumed Caryn's agency was handling the sale. From the sound of it, Caryn and the owners were friends, so maybe they'd decided to go with someone else rather than involve a friend in a financial matter.

"My guess is Nina didn't because she's engaged to Deidra's eldest son. I know when Gerald and I were engaged, I never would've said anything like that to his mother."

Juliette or anyone else not familiar with Caryn might find it odd that she offered up so much information about the current homeowners. He'd known Caryn and her family much of his life. If the woman hadn't shared so much additional personal info, it would have surprised him.

Caryn left them standing near the sauna and walked to the far end of the room. "The pool is saltwater." She pressed a button, and the blinds rose to reveal a wall of glass. On the other side was a manmade beach area and the lake. "This is one of my favorite rooms in the house. I just love the view."

He had to agree it was spectacular.

"I don't know if you can see it from where you're standing, but there's a boat dock at the end of the beach."

The house had an indoor pool and a sauna. Naturally, it

had a boat dock. Somewhere inside there was probably a private bowling alley.

After strolling through the home library that looked like it'd been ripped from the set of a Jane Austen novel, Caryn led them upstairs and through the six bedroom suites. Much like on the first floor, each room had its own unique decor style. A third-floor game room complete with a pool table and a wet bar rounded out the home's primary living areas. The crazy decorating scheme aside, if he had the money, he'd consider buying the place just to have the indoor pool and game room.

AARON PULLED up the contact number for Bruno's Pizza in his phone. After looking at the various properties, they'd headed back to the cottage to eat dinner. "Anything specific you want on the pizzas?"

"Not really," Juliette answered, looking up from the stack of paperwork in her folder.

Her response didn't help him much, especially since Bruno's had everything from a breakfast pizza covered with scrambled eggs and bacon to what they called the Belly Buster, an extra-large Sicilian-style pizza covered with fried chicken fingers, french fries, and mozzarella sticks. Personally, he couldn't imagine eating a pizza topped with such a combination, but he'd heard it was popular.

"Okay, are there any toppings I should avoid?" He'd eat almost any type of pizza set in front of him. He'd even eat anchovies in a pinch, but give him a pizza with pineapple and jalapeno peppers, a strange combination his sister loved, and he'd rather go hungry.

"I'm not a fan of black olives or broccoli on pizza." She went back to separating the paperwork into four piles, one for each of the properties they'd viewed. "You know what, if you don't mind, I'd love a pizza with sausage on it."

He loved meat of any kind on his pizza, so if she wanted sausage, he'd get one with it. "Do you want anything besides pizza?" He planned to order a side of onion rings. The combination might not make the healthiest of dinners, but so what? An unhealthy meal every once in a while never killed anyone.

Juliette added a plot plan to a pile and shook her head. "I'll eat whatever you get."

By the time he'd called in their order, she'd finished separating the paperwork and was reviewing one of the piles in more detail.

"The food should be here in about thirty-five to forty minutes." He took the empty seat next to her and glanced at the property disclosure she held. "Any thoughts about what we looked at today?" She hadn't said too much about any of the homes or the old dance studio.

"Except for all the pink, I like the old dance school. It's well laid out, there is adequate seating for parents who stay and wait for their children, and all the major areas were updated recently." She pulled out an interior and exterior diagram of the school from a pile. "And if I put an addition onto the building here, I could make a locker room so dancers have a place other than the bathrooms to change and a room for the teachers to relax or eat between classes." She gestured to the back-left corner of the building. "I might wait on that, though."

It sounded like she'd made up her mind about opening a business. "You're going to make an offer on the building then?"

"My mind was more or less made up before we walked into the place today. And I spent some time earlier today working on a business plan. I'd love to be able to open for the summer, but I'm not sure that's realistic, even if everything goes perfectly. But unless something unexpected comes up, it should be open for the fall, and that's when most dance schools start their new classes for the year anyway." Juliette returned the diagrams to the appropriate pile.

Whether or not she opened a business in town shouldn't matter to him. He'd known her only a few weeks, and during some of them, he'd kept his distance. But her ultimate decisions did matter, and not only because if she reopened the school his niece would once again have a place to do what she loved.

Nope, it had everything to do with her remaining in town because he enjoyed her company and wanted to see where this thing between them went, which would be next to impossible if she returned to Manhattan.

"I can't live in the dance school, though, so I'd like to find a house before I check out of here," she said, reaching a pile. "If I don't, I'll have to either rent this cabin for another few months or try to find something temporary nearby."

He left the running of the campground to Mom. But he didn't need to check the reservation system to know that this cabin, as well as the ones around her, might be available for a day or two here or there, but that was about it. People booked the cottages for the summer a year in advance.

But she could stay with him. It'd be easy enough to add a bed to the empty bedroom, and Candace could use his office if she needed a place to study.

"There's—" He stopped himself. They'd been in whatever this was for less than a week. Offering to let her stay with him was crazy. No, it wasn't crazy; it was insane. Especially since he no longer lived alone. Before he invited Juliette or anyone else he got involved with to move in, he needed to consider his niece.

"There's what?"

"Several motels in the North Conway area and a handful

of bed-and-breakfasts in Ashford, if you haven't closed on a house by the time you check out."

"I'm not worried about it."

Before he changed his mind and offered her the use of the spare bedroom, he better move the conversation along. "What did you think of the houses we looked at?" In terms of location, the eclectic Victorian took the number one spot in his book. Its spot on the lake rivaled his house's.

A playful smile tugged at the corners of her mouth as she rested her chin on her hand. "I think they all need a little more of the color pink inside."

He should keep his hands to himself, at least until they finished their conversation. Maybe even until after they ate. But with her so close and no one else around, he couldn't do it. Slowly, he brushed his fingers down her arm and over the top of her hand before threading them through hers. "Merry Baxter would probably agree with you there. Either she loves the color or the store had a good sale on pink paint the last time she painted the school. But seriously, did you like any of the houses today?"

"I loved the location and the overall floor plan of the one on Oak Ridge. The interior is another matter, but my cousin's wife is an interior designer. She would work wonders on the place. By the time she finished, you wouldn't even know it was the same house. And there I would have enough room for my family to visit."

He'd noticed the asking price on the house listing. Granted, it was a new house with an excellent spot on the lake, but it seemed ridiculous to spend so much on a place and then dump even more money into it. He was about to share his opinion when he remembered who he sat next to. Juliette might act like the girl next door, but she was as close to being that as he was to being the Tooth Fairy. She could hand over the ridiculous asking price, pay for any renovations, and not make a dent in her savings account.

"Remodeling takes time," he said instead.

"Yeah, but it's not like the house is uninhabitable as is. I could live there while the changes are being made."

"What about the house on Bedford Street?" Located on the Ashford side of the lake, the property's location wasn't as nice as the Victorian's and it wasn't as new, but at least the interior didn't look like a five-year-old had done the decorating.

She picked up the property listing and glanced over it. "The views of the lake aren't as nice, and the houses on either side are rather close. But I liked the inside a lot."

He'd rather not live in a house with neighbors so close. He'd done it when he lived in Boston, and given a choice, he'd never do it again. But Juliette called Manhattan home. He'd think she'd be used to having such close quarters. "It's also a lot older than the other two we looked at and smaller."

"The neighbors being so close bothers me more than the age of the house."

"No close neighbors on Cedar Road." Also in Ashford, the home on Cedar Road was almost as large as the first one they'd looked at and sat on six acres of land. Although not on the water, the landscaping around it almost made up for not being on the lake.

Juliette reached for the details of the final property. "I liked this one a lot too. But I do wish it was on the lake. Which one did you like better?"

Far too often, when a woman asked a man for his opinion, it didn't end well for the man. He'd rather avoid saying the wrong thing tonight. "It doesn't matter which one I liked. I don't have to live there." He lowered his head toward her neck as he spoke. "Which one do you like better?"

He kissed the skin just below her earlobe. Like when he'd

kissed her there last night, he heard her sharp intake of breath. Wanting to hear the sound again while at the same time not having to answer her question, he brushed his lips over the spot a second time.

"Are you trying to get out of giving me your opinion by distracting me?" she asked, placing her hand over the very spot he'd kissed.

So much for keeping silent on the issue. "Of course not."

Dropping her hand, she inched her chair away from him. "Good. Then which of the three did you like best?"

Well, if he had to answer, he'd be honest. "In terms of location, the first. As far as the house itself, I prefer the last." Aaron grabbed the back of her chair and pulled it closer to him again. "What about you?"

"At the moment, it's almost a tie between those two," she answered, her breath warm against his neck as she slipped her hand under his sweater and up his back. "The first one is closer to the dance studio." Her hand changed direction and snaked around to his chest. "And you."

Between her heat burning into his chest and her answer, his brain struggled to form an appropriate reply. Thankfully, she pressed her lips against his, making it impossible for him to speak anyway.

CHAPTER 14

LAST NIGHT, for the third straight Monday in a row, she'd joined him and Tiegan for dinner while Candace was at school. Aaron invited his mom over as well. Not surprisingly, she'd accepted. It had thrilled his mom when she learned they were together. In fact, he half expected her to already be collecting information on possible locations for their wedding reception. Candace and Tiegan had been pretty happy when they found out as well.

Once his mom left and Tiegan retreated upstairs to call friends, they'd moved into the living room and switched on the television. Although they'd settled on a show, they'd spent most of their time talking rather than watching the comedy. It'd been during their conversation the idea for today's outing came to him. Once he'd verified that Juliette didn't have any plans already and she left for the night, he'd gone back into his office and worked until almost eleven. Then he'd dragged his butt out of bed early this morning, skipped both his run and breakfast, and spent a few more hours tackling work. But now his work responsibilities were taken care of, and he could move on to more important things —a full day with Juliette all to himself.

After leaving his sister a note letting her know he wouldn't be around for dinner, Aaron put the cooler he'd packed and some blankets in his truck and drove down to the cottage.

Dressed for the day and holding a coffee mug, Juliette opened the door almost as soon as he knocked. "I thought I heard a car outside." She allowed him to enter and closed the door behind him. "What are you doing down here?"

They'd seen each other every day since the weekend the power went out and had developed somewhat of routine during the week. He spent the day in his office working. Around five or so, she'd either come up and spend a few hours with him and whoever else was in the house, or he'd go to the cottage. Unless he got a late start on his run and saw Juliette while she was out walking, they never saw each other at eight-thirty in the morning.

"Picking you up for the day. I hope you haven't eaten breakfast." If she had, he'd have to alter his plans.

"So far, I've only had coffee. Do you want some?"

He'd already had half a pot. He'd needed it when he climbed out of bed after only four hours of sleep. "Nope. I want you to grab a jacket and your boots. Probably your hat and gloves too." The forecast called for a gorgeous early spring day with temps in the high fifties. He'd rather play it safe, though.

"Uh, okay. But don't you have to work today?"

"Between last night after you left and this morning, I took care of everything."

"If you say so. I'll be right back."

True to her word, she didn't keep him waiting.

"Are you going to tell me where we are going, or should I guess?" she asked once they were on their way.

"The best breakfast place in New Hampshire. Possibly in New England." His favorite breakfast spot was only their first stop of the day.

"And that would be where?"

"Polly's Pancake Parlor." He'd never eaten better pancakes anywhere, and that included the ones his mom made. "I already called and had our name added to the waitlist."

"A waitlist for breakfast."

"The restaurant isn't large. Today it shouldn't be as busy, but in the summer, especially on the weekends, there is a two-hour wait to get a table."

Opened during the Great Depression, the popular restaurant had undergone some renovations a few years earlier, but it still resembled the place he'd started coming to before he could walk. While the owners served a full menu of breakfast foods and lunch options, Aaron couldn't imagine coming and ordering anything but their pancakes.

"I love the horse." Juliette gestured toward the red wooden horse outside the entrance, where two children sat while their mom snapped a picture.

"My mom must have at least a dozen photos of my sisters and me on its predecessor."

"Really?"

"Yep, every year she'd insist on taking a yearly picture of us on Trot Trot."

"I might have to ask her to see them. I bet you were an adorable five-year-old."

If a restaurant could be the embodiment of New England, it would be this place. When they'd walked in, they'd entered a small store that sold everything from pancake mix and real maple syrup to T-shirts and postcards. The store led directly into the dining room. Pictures of the family that started the business along with old New Hampshire license plates and farming tools from a bygone era decorated the wood-paneled walls.

Taking her seat, Juliette watched a server leave another table and enter the most unusual kitchen setup she'd ever seen. And she'd been in a lot of restaurants. As she watched, the server checked his pad and then reached for a metal funnel-shaped apparatus. The individual standing next to him did the same.

"What are they doing?" Polite or not, she pointed toward the employees.

He didn't even look over his shoulder. "Cooking pancakes."

Talk about an inefficient setup. No wonder there was a two-hour wait for a table on the weekends. "The servers cook the food?"

"Just the pancakes."

Interesting. Juliette switched her attention away from the kitchen to her menu. As Aaron promised, the restaurant had a variety of options. Since the place was called a pancake parlor, pancakes seemed the logical choice. "How does this work?" Several different pancake batters were listed along with numerous things you could have added to them.

Aaron added milk and sugar to the coffee their server set down along with a tray containing several maple products. "You can pick three different pancake batters or just one. Up to you. Then you choose up to three different add-ins. Our server will cook three pancakes and bring them out. When you're just about done with the first three, she'll bring out the rest. It's why the servers make the pancakes instead of the back kitchen."

"What are you having?"

"Gingerbread with walnuts, cornmeal with blueberries,

and oatmeal with coconut. I'm also getting a side of bacon and roasted potatoes. The pancakes aren't huge."

Yeah, she'd never finish six pancakes and two sides.

In the end, Juliette ordered four buttermilk pancakes, two with blueberries and two with walnuts, and the special pancake of the day, which consisted of bananas added to an oatmeal batter. She ordered a side of potatoes as well after Aaron promised to finish whatever food she couldn't.

She watched Brandy, their server, as she walked away and stopped at another table before going to the kitchen. Rather than start cooking like her counterparts around her, Brandy looked in Aaron's direction again. While talking their order, the woman hadn't been able to keep her eyes off him.

Look all you want, but he's with me. "What time did you get up this morning?"

"Three."

No wonder he'd had a travel mug of coffee with him in the truck. "And how long did you work after I left last night?" She'd kissed him goodnight and driven back to her cottage around nine.

"For about two hours."

"Four hours of sleep. Why would you do that? We could've come here some weekend."

Reaching across the table, he took her hands. "I wanted to surprise you."

"You could have surprised me on Saturday and got a few more hours of sleep."

Moving his thumbs across her palms, Aaron met her eyes as the rest of the room disappeared. "I couldn't wait until then to have a whole day alone with you."

If people didn't surround them, she would have leaned across the table and kissed him. With kissing off the table for the moment, she smiled.

When Brandy set down their order, he released her hands.

"Can I bring you anything else?" the server asked after she refilled Aaron's coffee.

Although Brandy spoke to him, he held Juliette's gaze. "I have everything I need here, thanks."

The words shot past her heart and plunged into her soul.

FOLLOWING BREAKFAST, they headed into the town of Lincoln and visited first the Basin located in Franconia Notch State Park. They stayed there watching the Pemigewasset River rush into the giant pothole-like formation that had existed for more than ten thousand years. Only when others joined them did they leave and drive to the next location on Aaron's itinerary.

Curt had mentioned the Flume Gorge, located in the same state park, while telling her about a day trip he'd taken with Taylor and her niece in the fall. She'd never considered taking the time to visit herself. The attraction itself didn't open until May, however, individuals could hike along the Ridge Path regardless of the month. And that was what they did. While more challenging than the walks she'd been taking through the campground, she loved every minute of it and looked forward to more hikes in the future.

Even after their hike, Aaron hadn't been done with surprises. After a leisurely drive along the Kancamagus Highway, they stopped at his favorite spot, a small parking area with a covered gazebo and an unobstructed view of the mountains. While she enjoyed her surroundings, Aaron covered the bed of his truck with blankets and laid out a late-afternoon picnic. Usually, when she ate outside, she did so on the deck of her cousin's beach house or under a tent with cloth napkins on the table. And those meals often consisted of filet mignon, not turkey and cheese sandwiches and potato chips. Even still, she'd never enjoyed a meal outside more. And it was all due to the man sitting next to her and, not surprisingly, yawning.

"Tomorrow, I'll call and make reservations for the three of us at Adventure Park this weekend," Aaron said, opening a thermos of coffee he'd packed. "Would you rather go on Saturday or Sunday?"

Although she'd suggested they take Tiegan to the indoor skydiving and surfing place weeks ago, they hadn't gotten around to it yet. "Whatever. It doesn't matter to me."

"I'll—" A yawn interrupted him, and he rubbed his eyes. "—try for Saturday."

"I think we should go."

"You're probably right. I'm sorry."

"Sorry? For what? Being tired?" Leaning into him, she touched her lips to his. "I don't blame you for being tired. I would be too. And while I had a fantastic day, next time don't get up so early just for me."

"As long as you enjoyed yourself, the missed sleep was worth it."

Words were great when you could find the appropriate ones. At the moment, she couldn't. With words off the table, she pressed her mouth against Aaron's again while she lost yet another piece of her heart to him. At the rate she was going, the whole thing would belong to him soon.

CHAPTER 15

AFTER PICKING up the various paint color cards, Aaron shuffled through them Friday night while waiting for Juliette to finish her phone call. He'd never realized there were so many shades of white, and to be honest, many of them looked the same to him. The same was true of the various purple cards. On the sofa next to him, Juliette thumbed through the catalog of light fixtures on the coffee table while she talked on the phone.

Although she didn't close on the property until the end of the month, ever since Merry accepted her offer three weeks ago, Juliette had been focused on her dance school. When she wasn't looking at paint colors or furniture for the office and waiting areas, she worked on a tentative class schedule with his sister. As he'd anticipated, Candace had signed on as soon as Juliette offered her a teaching position. Sandy had too. Only Lucy, another former teacher from Dance Dynamics, had turned down Juliette's offer. Not that it mattered in the long run.

Like he'd warned Juliette, much of the town knew not only that they were together but also that Juliette had looked at the building and was thinking about opening a new dance school even before Juliette made an offer on the property. Once word got out that she'd hired Sandy and Candace but needed a third teacher, his sister had received a call from one of her former dance students. The young woman, who worked as an X-ray technician at the immediate care in Danielson, missed dancing and wanted to teach. After talking to Candace and then meeting with the woman, Juliette hired her on the spot.

"Thanks, Addie. I'll see you guys tomorrow."

Aaron knew she'd mentioned the name to him at some point, along with several others, but he didn't remember if the woman Juliette spoke to now was a friend or a cousin. The woman had more cousins than anyone else he knew.

Setting aside the cell phone, she snagged a raw pepper from the platter and dragged it through the hummus. They'd both eaten late lunches, so they'd opted for snacks rather than a full meal when he arrived earlier.

"That was my cousin Trent's wife, Addie," she explained.

"The interior designer?" It was as good a guess as any.

"Mmm," she replied while she chewed.

While she'd called and made an offer on the dance school the day after they looked at the building, she'd checked out two other homes and some undeveloped land for sale before making an offer on the Victorian. When she did, they'd both expected the current owners to accept immediately. After all, Caryn claimed the owners were eager to sell, and according to her, it was the first offer they'd received since the house went on the market. They hadn't.

Instead, they came back with a ridiculous counteroffer. It'd taken about a week of going back and forth before they'd reached an agreement.

"Caryn arranged for us to go over to the house so Addie can see what she has to work with and start doing up some plans. Addie called to warn me that Trent is coming along. Since they're staying at my cousin Curt's house tonight and tomorrow, Curt's decided to come too. He's bringing his fiancée and Taylor's niece."

"Curt's the one who lives in New Hampshire?" He hadn't met the man, but he remembered one of her cousins lived to the south of Avon and had come to visit her at least once.

"Yes. He came up not long after I arrived." She marked the catalog page with a sticky note and closed it.

"How long do you think they'll stay?" Over the past several weeks, he'd grown accustomed to spending his weekends with her. He'd prefer not to go all day tomorrow without seeing her.

Juliette picked up the paint cards displaying the various shades of purple available and shuffled through them. "Probably most of the day. Why?"

Although comfortable for two people, the cottage wasn't designed for entertaining. Not to mention she'd met some of his family. He wouldn't mind getting to know some of hers, and he might not get another opportunity anytime soon, considering all except Curt lived out of state.

"You don't have a lot of room here. If you're interested, you can all hang out at my house after you go over to Oak Ridge. Or even before, depending on when Caryn's expecting you. And it's supposed to be a nice day, so I can cook outside on the grill."

When she didn't answer right away, he wondered if she wasn't ready to introduce him to her family. They spent so much time together over the past month that it often felt like they'd known each other a lot longer than they really had. If he stood in her position, perhaps he'd want to wait longer and see where things went before introducing her to his family.

Yep, maybe it'd been a dumb idea on his part. "If you'd rather not, it's okay. I won't be upset."

"It's not that." She wrapped her fingers around his wrist and gave it a gentle squeeze. "I was trying to decide whether or not it's fair to subject you to my cousins already. I adore them both, and we often treat each other more like siblings. Unfortunately, that also means they sometimes like to take on the role of overprotective older brothers, especially when my brother Scott's not around to do the honors. Trent and Jake are probably the worst about doing it. I think it's because they're the oldest of all the cousins. If they were the two coming tomorrow, you'd want some reinforcements around." She paused and then patted the top of his hand. "Even though Curt's not as bad as Jake, you'll still have Trent to deal with, so you might want some around anyway."

She looked serious, but the hint of humor in her voice made it hard for him to gauge how worried he should be about meeting some of the male members of her family. "I can make sure Candace and Tiegan join us. I think my mom has plans."

"As long as you're positive, I love the idea. And if Tiegan's there, it'll give Reese someone to hang around with. Taylor's niece is around Tiegan's age."

"I wouldn't have offered if I wasn't. There's a great butcher shop in Ashford. I'll head over there in the morning and pick stuff up. What time do you expect them?"

She set aside two of the paint cards and then went back to shuffling through the rest. She'd decided to go with a purple and white theme throughout the school. She'd already ordered a new purple awning to replace the pink one, although she hadn't actually called it purple. She'd referred to it as Majestic Plum. Whatever Juliette and the company making the awning wanted to label it, at the end of the day, he called it purple.

"They're planning to be here around noon. And we're

184

meeting Caryn at the house around one o'clock." She plucked another card from her stack and set it off to the side.

"Maybe you should stick with the pink. It might grow on you." Aaron selected a fat cherry tomato from the plate. "Who knows, after a few months of looking at it, you might even want to paint your bedroom a nice shade of bubble gum pink."

"Don't see that happening. I also don't feel like looking at this stuff anymore today." She set the cards down on top of the catalog and closed her laptop. Before he could do anything with the cards he held, she plucked them from his hand and set them aside too.

He'd spent the entire day sitting at his computer working. He'd be more than happy to hang around and do nothing for the rest of the evening. But if Juliette wanted to go out, he'd go. "You name it, and I'll do anything you want except for indoor surfing. There's no way I'm up for that tonight."

The previous weekend they'd taken Tiegan up to North Conway and spent the day at Adventure Park. He'd enjoyed the skydiving portion of the day. The jury was still out on the surfing part. He considered himself an athletic guy who picked up new things quickly. On Saturday, he'd spent far more time in the water than on his surfboard. Maybe he would have done better if his instructor had paid more attention to him than Juliette. It had pissed him off at the time, but he couldn't blame the guy for staring at her the whole time. Hell, he'd even had a difficult time keeping his eyes on the water and his brain off removing the plain one-piece bathing suit she wore. Naturally, by the time they left, Tiegan looked as though she'd been surfing for years and couldn't wait to go back.

"Next time we go, I'll be your instructor. You'll be surfing as well as Tiegan by the time we leave."

Not a chance. Forget about staring at her while in the

water, he'd be too busy trying to keep his hands off her to pay attention to anything she said. Even now, with her sitting there dressed in jeans and a T-shirt, he found it difficult to keep his hands off her.

"I'm where I want to be tonight." Earlier in the week, her nails had been painted a peachy color. The fingernails going across his arm now were light pink with bright white tips. She didn't pause when she reached his shoulder. "Well, more or less." The pads of her fingers lightly brushed across only the side of his neck, yet somehow he felt it everywhere.

More or less? What did she mean by that? Did she want to go back to his house? He certainly didn't at the moment. Tiegan had three of her closest friends from school over for the night. Unless he waited until two in the morning to go home, he'd find them awake in the living room watching television and eating every snack in the house.

Her lips replaced her fingertips. At first, they followed the same path, but when they reached his ear instead of making a return path toward the collar of his T-shirt, they moved along his jaw. By the time they reached his mouth, he almost didn't remember he wanted to ask her about her response. She teased his lips with a combination of short and long kisses before finally tracing her tongue across the seam of his lips and encouraging him to open for her.

If Juliette wanted control, he'd give it to her. He found he enjoyed letting her set the tone and pace from time to time. Closing his eyes, he lost himself in the taste of her and hoped he survived the kiss.

With his senses otherwise occupied, he didn't register that she'd moved until she straddled his lap. His body tightened, and whatever part of his brain still functioning turned itself off. Once the initial surprise of her position dimmed, he ran his hands up her thighs and to her waist. The tops of his fingers brushed against the skin just above the waistband of her jeans before she pulled away, ending their kiss.

Rather than speak, she held his gaze and moved against him. Groaning, Aaron tightened his hold on her waist, because he wouldn't survive if she kept moving against him like that. In return, Juliette smiled. Evidently, she enjoyed torturing men.

Her hands slipped off his shoulders and in the general direction of his hands. He assumed she intended to pull them away, or at least try, not that he'd let her succeed. Her hands never touched his. Instead, she grabbed the bottom of her T-shirt and pulled it over her head.

And he momentarily stopped breathing. As if it had a mind of its own, his hand covered her breast before dipping his finger underneath the dark blue lace and reclaiming her mouth.

Rather preoccupied, he barely registered she'd unclipped her bra until the material disappeared.

"I think this needs to go," she whispered against his lips while pinching his T-shirt between her fingers.

If she wanted his T-shirt gone, he'd happily oblige. Grabbing the collar of his shirt, he yanked it over his head. "If we're giving each other our opinions, I've got one," he said, slowly moving his index finger down her stomach toward her navel. He paused before going any farther, giving her a chance to tell him to stop or move away. She didn't do either.

"I'm listening."

Aaron reached down and grabbed the button of her jeans. "These need to go too."

Without saying anything, she moved off his lap, undid the row of buttons, and slipped the jeans down her hips. "Is there anything else you think needs to go?"

~

STARING AT THE CEILING, Aaron understood for the first time why some people referred to it as making love rather than having sex. He didn't have the most extensive dating history, but he'd had sex. Yet he couldn't lump his experience tonight with those from his past. It'd been more than the simple act of giving each other pleasure. Although they'd accomplished that. If she'd given him any more pleasure, his heart might have given out.

Then again, since so many other aspects of their relationship differed from his past ones, maybe he should have known sex with Juliette would be different too.

The memory of him telling Robby to get his head examined two years ago popped up. Considering that he had a beautiful woman naked next to him and using his chest as a pillow, Robby didn't belong in his thoughts. Still, the conversation they'd had after Robby announced he'd asked Madeline, a woman he'd known less than a month, to marry him continued. Robby insisted he loved her and knew she was the one.

Aaron, along with most of their other friends, assumed Robby and Madeline would get divorced within the year. People didn't fall in love at first sight or in a matter of days. Relationships that involved more than physical attraction took months. Even when time was involved, some never went past being physical. Despite everyone's doubts, the couple was not only still married, but they had a three-month-old daughter.

Propping herself up on an elbow, Juliette looked at him while the hand that seconds ago had rested on his chest touched his cheek. "I thought you'd fallen asleep."

Even after weeks of being around her, she occasionally took his breath away. And now was one of those moments. Unable to stop himself, he ran his fingers through her hair before tucking some behind her ear. "Nope. Just thinking."

Wrong choice of words. In Aaron's experience, when you

uttered those words to a woman, they started asking questions.

On cue, her eyebrows rose a fraction, and she asked, "About?"

I might owe my buddy an apology. Aaron had no plans of dropping to one knee and proposing to Juliette anytime soon. At the same time, he couldn't ignore that his feelings for her were deeper and more intense than he'd ever felt.

"Meeting your family tomorrow." He offered up the first excuse that came to mind. And in some ways, it wasn't a complete lie. He wasn't thinking about it now, but tomorrow before her cousins arrived, he would be. According to Juliette, Trent and Curt played the role of the protective older brother. He knew the role well. He'd played it often enough.

"Don't worry too much about them. Addie and Taylor will make sure they behave. And I'll be there to protect you." Lowering her head, she kissed him before she returned her hand to the center of his chest. "Would anyone notice if you spent the night here?"

With four eleven-year-old girls in the living room, his sister was upstairs, not sitting on the sofa waiting to make sure he came home. So as long he didn't walk through the door tomorrow at noon wearing the same clothes he'd left the house in tonight, he should be able to avoid drawing Candace's attention to the fact he'd spent the night. And Tiegan hadn't even seen him leave. She'd been too preoccupied with her friends, so for all she knew, he was already upstairs avoiding the madness that had taken over his living room.

"I doubt it."

She smiled, and an emotion he couldn't label expanded in his chest.

Yep, he might have been mistaken about the correlation between time and relationships.

"Stay here tonight. We can set an alarm so you can get home before everyone there wakes up."

He didn't need to hear her invitation a second time. "I left my phone downstairs." He kicked back the blankets. He couldn't set the device if he didn't have it. "I'll be right back."

THANKS to the moonlight coming through the windows and the light spilling into the room from the hallway, they hadn't bothered to shut the door when they came in the bedroom, so she could follow Aaron's movements as he stood. Other than run, she didn't know what type of exercise he did, but he clearly did something besides sit at his desk and stare at a computer screen. At the same time, it was apparent he didn't spend hours lifting weights every day.

She knew people, like Holly, who found men with bulging muscles and popping veins attractive. Not her. She'd always been drawn to men who, well, who were built like Aaron. He had phenomenal muscle definition, especially in his arms. Some women drooled over a sexy butt, and others went crazy for a chiseled six-pack. While she enjoyed seeing both, her eyes always went first to a man's arms. And Aaron's were perfect.

Once he left the room, she flipped on her back and let her mind wander. In March, she'd come to Avon to get away from the media attention and find a quiet place to make some decisions. At the time, if Holly or anyone else had suggested she should move here and open a business, she would've said not in this lifetime. Yet, it was exactly where she found herself. And she wouldn't have it any other way. Everything about her decision felt right. Almost as if karma had sent Daniel and the media drama associated with him into her life, so she'd take a break from the city and reassess her life.

Someday perhaps she'd have to send Daniel and his wife a thank-you note. If not for them, she might be in Manhattan right now, getting ready to go to another club or party and spend time with people she didn't care about.

Thanks to her disastrous relationship, though, she'd soon be doing something she loved again while spending her time with a man she liked. No, that wasn't quite right. She liked Aaron's sister and his mom. What she felt for Aaron was so much stronger.

I care about him. She couldn't put her finger on exactly why, but that sentiment didn't fit the bill either. Sophomore year of college, she'd been "in love." Back then, she'd thought she loved Paul. She had her doubts though because when he'd asked her to marry him, she'd told him she wasn't ready. He'd broken up with her then and there. If she'd truly loved him, the way her brother loved his wife, wouldn't she have given him a different answer even though she hadn't felt ready to get married? She had no idea, but she knew her feelings for Aaron differed greatly from what she remembered experiencing with Paul.

Was it possible she loved Aaron? They hadn't been together long. But in the end, did it matter how long she'd known him?

Aaron entered the room, and Juliette pushed the question to a back burner. You needed to work some things out when you were alone. Whether she loved Aaron already was most certainly one of them.

"I thought you might want one too." He held out one of the two bottles of water he'd brought back.

Until she spotted the water, she hadn't been thirsty. "Thanks."

Getting back into bed, he used the headboard as a backrest and opened his bottle. "You looked deep in thought when I walked in. Is everything okay?"

"Yeah, I was thinking about you."

It's not a lie. Juliette couldn't tell him she loved him, since she didn't know for sure. Not to mention, some guys acted weird when they heard the L-word. "Except for Addie, none of my family knows I'm seeing someone. Well, maybe Trent does. I didn't tell Addie not to tell him."

So what if it wasn't what she'd been thinking about when he walked in? She had thought about it early today when she talked to Mom.

He frowned, and she wondered if maybe she should have told him her mind had been on the dance studio instead.

"Huh, I'm not sure how I should interpret that, especially since you don't seem to care that everyone in town knows we're together. And I know you've talked to at least your mom several times over the past few weeks."

She had no problem telling him the truth on this one. "To say it pleased my mom when I told her I decided to leave modeling and open a dance studio would be an understatement. She's been after me for years to do something else. Mom would've preferred I either come work at the Helping Hands Foundation or take a position at Sherbrooke Enterprises, but she knows how much I love dance. And starting any type of business is better than standing in front of a camera, in her opinion."

"Okay, but what does that have to do with us?"

Her mom didn't know the particulars of Juliette's past relationships, but she knew they never lasted long. "I didn't want her to think I'd decided to stay here because of you."

"You were thinking about opening the studio before we got involved."

"You and I know that; no one else does."

A look of understanding crossed his face as he laced his fingers with hers. "I get it."

"But next time I talk to Mom, I'm going to tell her. And

next Friday night, my uncle is hosting a private fundraiser at his house in Weston for my uncle Warren. I'd like you to come with me. We can either stay at my parents' house, they live two streets over from my uncle, or at a hotel in Boston. Whatever you're more comfortable with."

She took it as a bad sign when Aaron didn't immediately respond. "I can handle a fundraiser," he answered, eventually squeezing her hand. "But I'm not sure about staying with your parents. I might just get myself a room in the city. I have an early morning meeting at the office next Friday anyway. Maybe I'll drive down Thursday afternoon and check into a hotel, and then I won't need to deal with traffic on Friday."

"I have the closing on Friday, so I can't drive down with you. But if you want, I'll stay with you at the hotel after the fundraiser. It might be nice to spend the weekend in Boston and come back on Sunday night."

Aaron brought her hand to his mouth and kissed her palm. "Sounds like a plan."

CHAPTER 16

WHEN JULIETTE HAD PACKED for her New Hampshire getaway, she'd included jeans and T-shirts, not cocktail dresses. Unfortunately, even though the fundraiser tonight was at her uncle's home, she couldn't show up in her favorite jeans. However, she had an entire wardrobe at her parents' house, since she visited so often, and it contained everything from bathing suits and sweaters to dresses perfect for a political fundraiser. That's why she'd planned to head to Weston after leaving Caryn's office. Plans were only good when executed, though.

The moment she had the keys to the dance school in her hand, she couldn't resist stopping by the building. Even as she'd unlocked the door, she'd promised herself she'd take a quick peek inside and then get on the highway. Once inside, she got carried away. Instead of taking a stroll through each room and locking the place back up, she started envisioning where she should place this piece of furniture she'd ordered or where to hang that picture she'd purchased. An hour after walking in the building, she finally dragged herself out.

Traffic made the two-and-half-hour drive from Avon to

Weston into an almost three-and-a-half one instead. When she finally arrived at her parents' house, she hadn't lingered over which outfit to wear. She grabbed the first suitable dress her eyes landed on before heading into Boston. When they spoke yesterday, Aaron had offered to swing by and pick her up before the fundraiser. She suggested meeting him at the hotel instead, because if he picked her up here, on Sunday when it was time to leave the city, he'd have to bring her back to her parents' house to get her car. But if she went to the city now, she could leave her car in the hotel parking garage and then on Sunday when they checked out, both their vehicles would already be in Boston.

Perhaps the same karma that sent her to Avon was at work because she pulled into the parking garage at the Sherbrooke Copley Square, where Aaron had been since last night, less than twenty minutes after leaving her parents' house—a rare event when it came to traveling to any part of Boston.

"You should've called when you got here. I would've come down and helped you with your bags," Aaron said when he answered the door.

She'd thought he couldn't look any sexier than he did in jeans. She'd been wrong. As Holly would say, the man was panty-melting hot in a suit and tie. Tonight he'd be getting the attention of women of all ages, which meant she'd have to glue herself to his side in case one of her uncle's guests decided to do more than look.

"I don't have much." She draped her dress over the back of a chair and turned toward him so she could give him a proper greeting. She concentrated on that and nothing else for several minutes. But when his fingers went under her shirt and unclipped her bra, she brought their kiss to an end. "If we don't stop now, I'm never going to want to leave."

The hands still on her back sneaked around and covered her breasts. "And that's a bad thing?"

"Yes and no. I don't care much about the fundraiser, but I want you to meet my family."

The previous weekend, he'd met Trent and Curt. At first, Aaron had seemed a little uncomfortable, but within no time, the three of them were getting along like old friends. While the guys discussed sports and some video game she'd never heard of, she'd shared her plans for the dance school with Addie, Taylor, and Candace, who had fit in perfectly with the group. Even Tiegan and Reese had hit it off immediately. In fact, they'd been inseparable the entire day.

As much as she enjoyed having Aaron's hands on her bare skin, she reached under her top and pulled them away, since he didn't look like he had any intentions of moving them. "We don't have to stay until the end." She reclipped her bra as she spoke. "I promise we'll just hang around long enough for you to meet my family, and then we'll come back here for the rest of the night. Once we come back, we don't have to leave the suite again if you don't want to. We can get room service and stay in bed for the rest of the weekend."

"Sounds like an excellent idea to me." He glanced at his watch before shoving his hands in pockets. "Unless you want to be late, you probably should get changed. It's already five, and traffic out of the city on Friday nights is ugly."

Good idea or not, she dropped a kiss on his cheek before grabbing her dress.

"I'll wait out here. If I come in there with you, we won't be going anywhere tonight."

An hour later, they were sitting in traffic on the Mass Turnpike. She'd never minded traffic all that much. After all, living in New York City, it was merely a part of life. But after being in Avon for over a month, where getting stuck behind the school bus was the worst of the traffic, she found it beyond irritating.

"The uncle that's hosting the fundraiser is your mom's brother?" Aaron asked.

"Right. My mom has three older brothers. We're going to Uncle Jonathan's house. He's Curt's father. You'll also meet my uncle Mark, Trent's dad, tonight." She loved all of her uncles, but Uncle Mark had always been her favorite. Although exactly why, she couldn't say.

She'd considered offering to drive, but when Aaron offered first, she'd happily handed over the keys to her car and climbed in the passenger seat. "You want to take the next exit."

Aaron switched on the car's directional light and waited for an opening in the other lane. "What about President Sherbrooke? Will he be there?"

Even after more than three years, she found it strange to hear people refer to her uncle as President Sherbrooke. Maybe it wouldn't seem so odd in another three, assuming he won a second term in November, which it looked like he would. "No, Uncle Warren won't be there tonight. But he'll be at my cousin Allison's wedding, so you'll meet him and Aunt Elizabeth then."

"I'm going to a wedding?" He moved into the other lane and then briefly glanced in her direction. "Where and when is this wedding I'm going to?"

She couldn't tell if he sounded amused or annoyed. "You don't *have* to go. But I'd like you to come with me."

Reaching over, he took her hand, squeezed it, and then placed it on his thigh. "I'm giving you a hard time. If you want me there, I'll come. Just tell me where and when."

"It's in June at Uncle Mark's estate on Martha's Vineyard."

"I've gone to Block Island three or four times but never Martha's Vineyard," he said, taking their exit off the highway and approaching a stop sign. "Which way now?"

"Left, and at the traffic light take a right. We should be there in about five minutes."

Fundraisers and other society events didn't faze her; she'd simply been to too many of them over the years. While each one might be for a different purpose, they all shared things in common, including the people on the guest lists. And some of those people were ones she only interacted with when given no other choice. The first person she spotted after walking into her uncle's house fell into that category. Before Tasha spotted her and either dragged her into a conversation or, worse, started hitting on Aaron—the woman was like a tiger stalking its prey when she saw a hot guy—Juliette took Aaron's hand and hurried in the opposite direction in search of her parents.

WHILE SITTING NEXT to her at the cottage or eating dinner with her at his house, Aaron forgot Juliette wasn't like everyone else he knew. When he kissed her, it never occurred to him that the woman in his arms came from one of the country's wealthiest families or that she called President Sherbrooke Uncle Warren. No, when they were together, she was just Juliette Belmont, the woman opening a new business in town and taking over his heart.

With the truth all around him, he couldn't forget or ignore it.

Aaron remained silent as she led him down another hallway and into a home library after speaking with her parents. Men dressed in custom-tailored suits and women wearing diamonds the size of golf balls sat chatting away inside. Thankfully, not only did he know four of the room's inhabitants, but he liked them. He hoped the rest of Juliette's family was as friendly and down-to-earth as the cousins he'd met last weekend.

The man standing near Curt looked in their direction as they entered and smiled. Aaron never wasted his time reading trashy tabloid magazines. Still, he'd seen the man's face enough times over the years while standing in the supermarket check-out line to know the individual next to Curt was Jake Sherbrooke, President Sherbrooke's son.

"We were just talking about you," Jake said in place of a proper greeting, hugging Juliette when they joined the group.

"No, we weren't," a pretty redhead commented, giving Juliette a hug once her cousin moved away.

"Don't worry, Juliette, Charlie is right. We weren't talking about you; we were talking about Aaron," Trent said with a grin.

"Just ignore them. It's what I do. Especially that one." The woman named Charlie pointed toward Jake, then extended her hand. "It's nice to meet you, Aaron."

Nodding, Juliette slipped an arm protectively around his waist. "It's what we all do."

"Funny, you weren't ignoring me this morning, Charlie," Jake said with a slight shrug before looking back at Aaron. "I hope my cousin treats you better than my wife treats me. Although knowing my cousin, it's debatable."

She'd told him her cousins Jake and Trent had similar personalities. From what he'd heard so far, it was true. "Juliette has her moments. But most of the time, she behaves."

Juliette pinched his side but didn't respond to his comment. "Are Scott and Paige here?"

"No. They decided to play it safe and not come," Jake answered.

"Makes sense." Juliette sounded disappointed as she accepted a glass of wine from a passing waiter and offered it to Aaron before taking one for herself.

During one of their many conversations, Juliette had shared her sister-in-law was pregnant with twins and due in June. He knew next to nothing about what pregnant women should or shouldn't do, but traveling seemed like something you might want to limit once you reached a certain point.

"Are Courtney and Josh here?" Juliette asked.

For the next moment or two, Curt gave her a rundown of what relatives were in attendance. After that, the conversation turned to Juliette's new business venture as well as her future home and the changes it needed. Eventually, they made their way to the large tent set up outside. Considering he'd so far spotted Governor Wentworth, Congresswoman Janice Bettencourt, Drew McKenzie, the star quarterback for the New England Rebels football team, and actor Anderson Brady among the guests tonight, he could only imagine the conversations that were going on around him.

No sooner did Juliette sit in the chair he'd pulled out for her than she stood back up. "All of you be nice," she said, looking at her three male cousins and then at him. "I'll be right back. I just want to say hello to Tory." She kissed his cheek before heading across the dance floor.

His eyes, along with those of several of the other male guests in attendance, followed her every movement. Without realizing it, he pushed back his chair so he could follow her and make sure everyone there knew who she'd be leaving with tonight.

"Wow, you've got it bad." Jake's voice stopped him before he stood. "But you've got nothing to worry about. My cousin hasn't taken her eyes off you all night. Don't you agree, Trent?"

Trent frowned and nodded. "Yeah, I wish someone would look at me the way Juliette's been looking at you, Aaron." In return, his wife pinched his hand. "Hey, that wasn't nice."

"Ignore the kids, Aaron. After a while, they'll be quiet," Curt said.

Aaron suppressed a smile but couldn't resist joining in the fun. "Do they always invite children to these types of things? Or is tonight a special occasion?" Although he hadn't expected to, he liked Juliette's cousins, at least all the ones he'd met so far.

"Unfortunately, these two are usually included." Curt pointed to his cousins.

"Charlie and I can't find babysitters willing to put up with them," Addie added.

He couldn't help but laugh. He'd been a little apprehensive about coming tonight, but it was turning into a very enjoyable evening.

"Next weekend, Taylor, Reese, and I are heading down to my house in Newport. You and Juliette should come down and join us. Tiegan's welcome as well. Reese keeps asking when she can see her again. And I promise Trent and Jake won't be there."

It'd been years since he'd been to Newport. A weekend down there would be nice. "Let me—" His eyes landed on a twentysomething-year-old man with light brown hair and a smug smile entering the tent, and the world around him came to a screeching halt. There was no way it could be who he thought it was. Tugging at his tie, he moved the knot down a fraction of an inch and watched the guest head toward the bar in the corner.

"Aaron, are you okay?" Trent still sat next to him. He could see Juliette's cousin from the corner of his eye, yet Trent's voice sounded as if he stood in another room.

"Who's the guy standing at the bar?" Somehow Aaron got the question out.

"Which one?" Trent asked.

"The twentysomething-year-old with light brown hair and

a gray suit." No, he had to be wrong. It couldn't be the same guy.

"Isn't it one of Prescott Casella's sons, Curt?" Trent asked.

Somehow Aaron remained seated as he watched the bartender hand a drink to the man in question.

Curt glanced over his shoulder and then back at the table's occupants. "Yeah. That's his youngest son, Bryon." Juliette's cousin didn't sound all that pleased to see the man either. "The Casellas live next door. I'm surprised Bryon is here, though. The guy is... let's just say not the type of person I'd want around my sister."

He hadn't noticed Juliette coming toward their table, but now she was sitting down next to him. "Who are you talking about?"

"Bryon Casella," Curt answered. "If he's here, I'm sure his parents are too."

"I passed them when I went over to see Tory. They were talking to your mom and mine."

Not only was the punk who'd killed his cousin here but the parents who helped him get off with little more than a slap on a wrist sat under the same tent as him. Perhaps even worse than being at the same event with the three of them was the fact they were guests of Juliette's family.

With no destination in mind, Aaron pushed back his chair. Before he went over and caused a scene, he needed to get away. "Please excuse me."

"Aaron, are you okay?" She reached for his hand, but he pulled it away before their fingers touched and stood.

"I just need some air."

"Air? We're outside?"

He didn't wait to see if Juliette followed him. He passed by the table where Governor Wentworth sat talking to one of the owners of the New England Rebels football team.

Exiting the tent, he crossed the well-manicured lawn. Behind him, he heard Juliette call out to him, but he didn't stop. He headed up the same stone walkway he'd walked down while joking with her family earlier and into the house.

Juliette grabbed his hand and tugged, forcing him to stop before he got any further. "Are you feeling okay? You look awful all of a sudden."

"I'm not sick." He tugged at his tie again. He needed to get away.

"Okay," she said slowly. "Then what's the matter?"

He didn't want to have this conversation at all and certainly didn't want to have it where anyone might come along and overhear. Taking in a deep breath, he exhaled slowly. "I cannot talk about it right now." He was probably being the biggest ass in history, but he couldn't help it. "I need to go. I'm sorry."

He saw the confusion and concern reflected in her eyes as she nodded. "Yeah, okay. We can go. Do you want me to drive?"

Did he want her to drive? He wasn't even sure he wanted her coming with him. Aaron shook his head rather than tell her the truth. "No, thanks."

CHAPTER 17

As much as she wanted to question him, Juliette kept her mouth shut on the ride back to the hotel. For the life of her, she couldn't figure what the problem was. She thought they'd been enjoying themselves, at least as much as anyone could at a political fundraiser. And while her cousins could be annoying—even she sometimes wanted to gag them all— they'd never do or say anything to make anyone react the way Aaron had. So that brought her back to her original question. Why had Aaron suddenly decided he needed to leave? And why couldn't he talk about whatever the problem was while at her aunt and uncle's house? Much of the house was off-limits to the other guests but not her. They could have found a quiet area upstairs and talked. Maybe if they had, they could've rejoined the party, and she would have gotten a chance to introduce Aaron to more of her relatives. Other than Jake and his wife and her parents, she'd only briefly introduced him to Aunt Judith as they passed her in the hall when they first arrived.

After opening the door to their suite, Aaron followed her inside. The moment they'd gotten in her car, he'd undone his tie and left it draped across his neck. Now, he pulled it off and tossed it on a nearby chair. His jacket followed the tie.

"You probably wanted to stay," he said, speaking for the first time since they left. "I'm sorry. If you want to go back, you can. You don't need to stay here with me."

He no longer looked shell-shocked. Juliette didn't know of any other word to describe how he'd looked earlier. But something had caused his earlier reaction, and she wanted to help him if she could.

"No, not really. I'd rather be with you." Unsure of how he'd react if she touched him, she moved closer but kept her arms by her side. "Is everything okay? You seemed upset at my uncle's house. Do you want to talk about it?"

Aaron raked a hand down his face and then through his hair. "You'd be...." Rather than continue, he paused and closed his eyes. When he opened them, the pain she saw almost knocked her to the floor.

"My cousin Troy and I were close. Much the same way you are with your cousins. Seven years ago, your uncle's neighbor Bryon Casella had a whole cocktail of drugs and alcohol in his system when he killed my cousin in a car accident. Troy's girlfriend survived, but she spent weeks in the hospital and then months going to physical therapy. Bryon and his sister walked away unharmed."

What did she say to that? "I'm sorry" didn't come close to being adequate, but what else was there? "I'm so sorry, Aaron. I can't even imagine how you must have felt." She couldn't even begin to imagine losing her siblings or cousins in a similar fashion.

"Do you know how much time Bryon spent in jail?"

She didn't know, and by the tone of Aaron's voice, she didn't want to either. "No."

"None. He had his license suspended and got probation. And you know why, don't you?" Even if she'd had a response, he didn't give her a chance to offer it. "Because money can buy just about anything, and his parents had plenty of it."

Hugging him might not be the right move, but she didn't know what else to do. He didn't push her away, but he didn't put his arms around her like he usually did either.

"I couldn't stay there and be around him."

She understood that. In a similar position, she would have left too. "I've bumped into Bryon at parties and whatnot, but I don't know him well. You won't have to see him again, I promise."

Aaron laughed sarcastically, sending an uneasy chill down her spine. "Great, I just have to be around people like him and his family."

People like him? How should she interpret that? And did she even want to know? Before she made up her mind, either way, he stepped away from her.

"You know what? I need a little time alone." He ran his fingers through his hair again. "I'm going to change and go downstairs for a swim. I'll be back in a little while."

Sometimes you needed to be alone. She understood that too, at least intellectually. Emotionally was another matter. "Okay. I'll be here."

She waited on the sofa while Aaron went into the bedroom and changed. Once he left, she went in and put on the pajamas she'd packed. She didn't bother to hang up her dress before pulling back the blankets and climbing into the king-sized bed. Earlier in the evening, she'd imagined climbing into it with Aaron while wearing far fewer clothes. Instead, she was flipping through the television stations while Aaron went for a swim. Talk about the night not going as she'd expected.

After going through all the channels more than once, she settled on a history channel and tossed the remote on the nightstand. They shouldn't have gone tonight. If they'd stayed in Avon, he never would've seen Bryon or the Casellas. Perhaps someday, in the distant future, he would've still told her about his cousin. However, doing so might have been less painful if he hadn't just seen the man responsible.

Be around people like him. Aaron's words repeated in her head while the narrator on the television talked about the building of Stonehenge. She wanted to believe he meant people who used their money to get out of trouble. And no question about it, people like that existed. In fact, she'd bet Bryon's family wasn't the only one at the fundraiser guilty of doing it.

The large knot in her stomach suggested her interpretation wasn't accurate. "It'll be fine." Maybe if she heard the words, not only thought them, she'd believe them. "Aaron just needs some time alone."

She heard the suite door open, and soon after, Aaron entered the bedroom with a towel draped over his shoulders. The frown he'd worn when he left remained fixed in place, and the knot in her stomach grew.

"How was your swim?" Not even the threat of torture would get her to ask the question really on her mind.

"Not bad. I had the pool to myself." He grabbed clothes from his suitcase and headed toward the bathroom. "I'll be right back."

Her cell phone on the nightstand chimed, and a glance at the screen revealed a text from Addie asking if everything was okay.

Beats me. Juliette kept the thought to herself and instead sent Addie a simple yes.

"We can look for something else to watch or turn the television off. It's up to you," Juliette said when Aaron came back into the room. She'd seen Stonehenge, and while it was an impressive structure, she didn't care about what part of

England the stones came from or how the builders transported them.

Aaron climbed into bed and repositioned his pillows behind him. "Do you mind putting on the baseball game? The Red Sox are playing the Angels in Los Angeles tonight."

Yep, she hadn't imagined watching the Red Sox play tonight, but if that's what he wanted, she'd put the game on.

FOR A LONG TIME, Aaron had stared at the ceiling, unable to fall asleep. When he finally did, it hadn't been a restful sleep. Instead, the memories from Troy's funeral and Bryon's trial plagued him. Thankfully, he hadn't stayed asleep long. Rather than linger in bed, he went into the other room and turned on game one of the 1986 World Series. It'd been either the game or a documentary about the Giza Plateau. Not that it mattered much in the long run what he put on, because he didn't pay much attention to the television. Even if it'd been this year's World Series and his favorite team had been playing, his thoughts would have remained focused on the events of the previous evening and the woman sleeping in the other room.

Over a month ago, when Candace pushed him to invite Juliette over, he'd admitted he would've considered it if she was like so many of the guests who stayed there. But since she wasn't, he had wanted nothing to do with Juliette, because people like her lived in a world that played by a different set of rules. The weekend the power went out, and she stayed with him, he began to see her more as someone he genuinely liked and enjoyed spending time with and less as an individual who had the money and influence to get away with anything—even the killing of another person. At some point between then and now, she'd gone from being someone he enjoyed spending time with to someone he cared about.

Not only did he care about her, but for the most part, he never thought about the influential people she was related to or the connections she had. Unfortunately, that started to change last night when they walked into her aunt and uncle's house. Seeing Bryon and knowing his parents were not only there but also her aunt and uncle's neighbors drove home the knowledge that Juliette existed in a part of society far removed from him. A part he'd have to put up with if he stayed in Juliette's life, and honestly, he didn't know if he could do it even for her. Until he reached a decision, it was probably in both their best interests to take a break from each other.

Aaron raked his hand across his hair. Yeah, if he couldn't get past who Juliette was and the people she associated with, then letting their relationship continue wasn't fair to her. While it might be the right thing, it sure as hell wasn't a conversation he wanted to have. Or one he ever expected to have.

Maybe I should have dropped off the wood. If he'd brought in the firewood and showed her how to use the wood-stove that Saturday afternoon back in March, perhaps he wouldn't be sitting here this morning. "A little late now." He dropped his head back against the sofa.

"Hey, have you been up long?"

Counting to five, Aaron reminded himself he was only doing what was best for both of them and looked at her. Last night, wearing a dress that looked as if it'd been made just for her and probably cost more than he made in a month, it'd been easy to remember people everywhere knew who she was and that her family owned one of the largest hotel chains in the world. Right now, wearing shorts and a top that read Not Until After Coffee, she could have easily been someone he'd met while eating lunch at George's Diner or bowling.

"Yeah, I've been up since about three o'clock."

"You're going to be exhausted later."

He knew it wasn't the only problem he'd have later.

"I'm going to make myself some coffee. Do you want some?"

Caffeine wouldn't make what he needed to say any easier, but it wouldn't hurt anything either. Plus, it'd buy him a little more time. *Coward.*

"Yes, please." He watched her walk into the kitchenette and switch on the single-serve coffee maker.

"Looks like we have dark roast and a breakfast blend. Do you have a preference?"

As long as it wasn't decaf, which in his opinion was just a step above dirty water, he'd drink anything. "It doesn't matter to me."

Sooner than he wanted, Juliette handed him a coffee cup and sat down next to him.

"Have you ever been to Emilia in the North End?"

Aaron sipped his coffee before he answered. "I don't think so."

"It's up to you, but I thought we could eat breakfast here and then make reservations there for dinner." She didn't wait for him to comment before opening the room service menu. "What do you think you want to eat this morning?"

Stop stalling. Waiting until he finished his coffee or ate breakfast wouldn't change what he needed to say. He took one last gulp of coffee and set his cup down. "We need to talk."

Pressing her lips together, she set aside the menu. "About last night? Aaron—"

He tried never to interrupt a person, but he did it now anyway. "Last night, I realized how different our lives are." Since he didn't know how to explain without sounding like the biggest ass, he'd do the best he could as he went along. "Your family owns one of the biggest hotel chains in the world. You have one uncle who lives in the White House, and another who hires valets to park cars at his private house party. I don't know your address in Manhattan, but it's probably somewhere on Billionaire's Row."

"What you said about my family is true, and I can't change it. But soon I'll be living and working in Avon. So the other stuff doesn't matter."

For how long? The question popped up in his head again. Like in the past, he pushed it aside. "I know, and I'm not asking you to change. But last night's fundraiser won't be the last event like that you'll need to attend. In June you've got your cousin's wedding. I can only imagine the names on the guest list. And I doubt any of them work as a cybersecurity engineer while sharing a house with their sister and eleven-year-old niece."

"My cousin's fiancé is one of Addie's older brothers and a Marine. Their three older brothers are also in the military, so I think the guest list will be more diverse than you think, Aaron."

Perhaps he deserved her slightly sarcastic tone. "I didn't know that." Hoping to dislodge the baseball stuck in his throat, Aaron swallowed.

"Not—"

"Not everyone is like the Casellas. I know, but it doesn't change the fact you and your family are used to a very different lifestyle than I am. And I'm not sure it's right for me." The baseball in his throat turned into a softball. "Believe me. This isn't easy. Part of me wants to lock us in the suite and not come out again until tomorrow. But I need time to figure out if—"

This time she cut him off. "You want me in your life."

He loved having her in his life. "No, if I can fit into yours. There's a huge difference there."

Juliette sighed and brushed away the moisture gathering

in her eyes. "Fair enough. I'll change and leave. Maybe I'll stay at my parents' house for the rest of the weekend." Standing, she picked up her coffee. "I'll be gone in a few minutes."

She walked past him, and the unshed tears in her eyes tugged at his heart.

"Juliette, I…." He stopped before he told her to forget everything he'd said. Before he told her he loved having her in his life. Maybe even loved her. If he uttered any of those words, perhaps she'd sit back down and kiss him. And at least for the weekend, they'd both be happy. But it wouldn't solve the problem of whether or not he could fit into her life.

"I'm sorry. And you're more than welcome to stay here. I can go."

Both Candace and Mom knew of his and Juliette's plans for the weekend. If he arrived home this afternoon alone, he'd get a lecture and a half from both of them. Much like him, they cared about Juliette and enjoyed having her a part of their lives. If they thought he'd somehow hurt her, which, based on her expression, he had, they'd be pissed at him.

She brushed her fingers across her eyes again and seemed to consider his offer. "No, I… um… I'll stay with my parents or maybe my sister in Providence tonight and then drive back to Avon tomorrow."

Fifteen minutes later, Juliette left, taking not only her suitcase but also a piece of his heart with her. If he'd had workout clothes with him, he would have headed out for a run. For whatever reason, running always helped clear his head so he could focus. And now more than ever, he needed to focus. Since he couldn't run, he changed into his bathing suit and headed down to the hotel pool. Maybe if he got lucky, it'd be empty. But he wasn't counting on it after the way the weekend had gone so far.

. . .

NUMEROUS TIMES, Juliette had given a boyfriend the it's-not-you-it's-me speech. Until today, she'd never been on the receiving end of it. Then again, she was the one who'd always ended her past relationships. And while she might not admit the actual number to anyone, she'd dated a lot of men. But she'd never cared about any of them the way she did Aaron.

Love, you mean. Ignoring both the thoughts and the hand squeezing her heart, she jabbed the elevator button marked lobby even though she'd rather march back down the hall and jab Aaron. Maybe if she jabbed him a few times, he'd get his common sense back.

Seriously, he didn't know if he could fit into her life because of who her family was and who they associated with? Maybe if her family resembled one of the mafia families portrayed in the movies, she could understand his reluctance. And she'd give him that sometimes she interacted with people she'd rather not be in the same room with. But everyone had to do it from time to time. It was merely part of being an adult.

When the elevator doors opened, she stepped out. Before, her first thought had been to stay at her parents' house for the night. But she didn't need to be in Avon at all this week. She could spend a night or two at her parents' or a few days visiting her sister. She could even go back to New York until the following week.

"Juliette."

Preoccupied with her and Aaron's conversation and where she should spend the next few days, she didn't see Anderson Brady until she almost walked into him. She'd known the actor for what seemed like forever, and they often attended many of the same parties. At one time, she'd even considered pursuing a romantic relationship with him, but whenever she'd been single, he'd been with someone and vice versa.

"Anderson, how are you?"

"Good. I thought I'd see you at the fundraiser last night." Much like his father, Anderson was a big supporter of Uncle Warren.

She'd spotted him taking to Drew McKenzie and his wife and had planned to go over and say hello at some point and introduce them all to Aaron. "I was there, but something came up, and I had to leave early."

"I'm going to be in Boston until Tuesday. Are you going to be around?"

"No, I'm checking out." Well, maybe checking out wasn't totally accurate, but she was leaving the hotel.

The cell phone in his hand rang, and he glanced at the screen. "I need to take this. But I'll call you when I get back to New York, and we can get together."

Yesterday she would have told him she had a boyfriend. Now, she nodded. "I'll see you later."

An hour and a half later, Juliette found herself not at her parents' house but instead at the Hillcrest in Providence and riding the private elevator up to Trent's penthouse—not that it had been her original destination after leaving the hotel. When she'd headed for Providence, she'd planned to visit her sister and her husband. She'd talked to Courtney on the phone, but she hadn't seen her since the wedding in February. Unfortunately, no one was home when she arrived at Courtney's place. When she called her sister, Courtney informed her they were picking up Josh's daughter and would be back later. Although she had a key, and Courtney insisted she let herself in, she felt uncomfortable doing so. Coming and going as she pleased when her sister lived alone had been one thing, but Josh lived there now. So rather than go in, Juliette called the first person who came to mind—Addie.

"I thought Aaron would be with you," Addie said, hugging Juliette after she walked inside.

"No. He's still in Boston." Well, she assumed he was. Maybe he'd checked out too and gone home.

"Oh." The why hung in the air, but before Juliette could explain, Trent walked in, his almost two-year-old son Kendrick perched on his shoulders. Jake was right behind him with his own mini-me in his arms, and it was evident they'd all been downstairs swimming.

"Hey, what are you doing here?" Trent asked.

"Visiting."

"I can see that. Where's Aaron? Based on the way you two were looking at each other, I figured you'd spend the weekend locked up in your hotel room."

"We had a slight change in plans."

Trent looked at his wife and then back at her. "Is everything okay? Aaron looked upset last night, and when you rushed out, we were all worried."

"It's complicated," she admitted. "Can I get something to drink? All I've had today is a few sips of coffee."

"Of course. You can have whatever you want," Addie answered.

"I'll be back after Kenrick and I are changed," Trent said.

Five years ago, if anyone had told her Trent and Jake, two of the worst playboys in the world, would both be happily married and fathers, she would have told them it would never happen. Yet, that was precisely the case. Not only that, but neither of them had ended up with society women. Instead, they'd both fallen for women who didn't have powerful connections or wealthy family members. Actually, Addie, Charlie, and Curt's fiancée, Taylor, had backgrounds similar to Aaron's.

She'd never asked any of them simply because it'd never occurred to her, but she wondered if they'd struggled the same way Aaron was now.

Addie followed her into the kitchen but remained silent as Juliette poured herself a large glass of lemonade.

She drank down half the glass and then refilled it. "Is Charlie here too?"

"Yes. They spent a few days in North Salem with her family and are staying here until Monday."

"Good. Hopefully, the two of you can help me with something." Nothing she did would change Aaron's feelings or his ultimate decision, but she'd like a better understanding of where he was coming from. Addie and Charlie might be able to give her that.

She'd just started sharing the reason they rushed out the previous night with Charlie and Addie when Trent and Jake entered the room with their sons. While her cousins joined them, their sons immediately forgot about the adults in the room and went to the train table.

"I'm not sure I would have been able to just walk out last night if I'd been in his place," Trent commented, speaking for the first time since sitting down.

Jake nodded in agreement. "Last night makes a lot more sense. But I thought the two of you were spending the weekend in Boston."

The fist around her heart squeezed tighter as she filled them in on what transpired this morning.

"What do you need Charlie and me to help you with?" Addie asked when Juliette finished.

"Understanding his problem with our family. It's not like we're all part of a cult."

Addie and Charlie exchanged a look, one she couldn't decipher.

"Being a part of this family takes some getting used to," Charlie said.

"That's one way to put it," Addie agreed, drawing her husband's attention her way. "Don't give me that look, Trent.

Your family isn't exactly like most, and you know it." She looked back over at her. "Some people might have a hard time fitting in."

"Then, you both had reservations about being with my cousins?"

Charlie conveniently took a sip of lemonade at that exact moment, leaving Addie to answer first.

"In a way, but not so much because of your family. It had more to do with Trent's reputation. Before we met, I'd see pictures of him on magazine covers with a different woman every week when I went to the store. Not exactly the type of person you get involved with if you want a serious relationship."

Trent put his arm around Addie and kissed her temple. "I didn't realize my reputation bothered you so much back then."

"I tried not to think too much about it in the beginning. And later, we had other issues to deal with."

Juliette didn't know what issues Addie referred to, but clearly, they'd worked them out.

"Jake's reputation was more of an issue than his family for me too. Well, that and getting used to the media attention."

"If you want, I'll tie him to a chair and force him to listen to me telling him about what a great family this is until he comes to his senses. And believe me, with four brothers, I can tie a knot he'll never get out of," Addie said.

"I'll help you," Charlie added.

Jake glanced at his cousin. "Trent, remind me never to make our wives mad."

"You have no idea." Trent's comment earned him an elbow in the side.

"Don't waste the money buying rope, Addie. I recognize the signs. Aaron is in love with Juliette already. The poor guy just hasn't realized it. He'll be knocking on her door in a couple of days and asking her to forgive him," Jake said.

"I can't believe I'm saying this." Trent looked like he'd bitten into a lemon. "But Jake's right, Juliette."

It might be unique, and its members definitely drove her crazy, but she wouldn't trade her family for any other. "Maybe we—" Her ringing cell phone interrupted her, and she dug the device out of her purse on the floor. Pressing the green icon on the screen, she greeted her mom.

"Paige's water broke. Your dad and I are on our way to New York."

Given the circumstances surrounding her nephew's birth, she hadn't met Scott's son until he was over a month old. It wasn't going to be the case this time. "I'll see you there."

CHAPTER 18

TUESDAY AFTERNOON, Aaron walked back up toward his house for the second time that day. Hoping to catch her before she headed over to the dance school or went out to take care of some other errand, he'd walked down to Juliette's cottage around nine o'clock. When he didn't see her car, Aaron assumed he would see her when she came back, and he returned home to work—or try to work. His mind had other ideas, much like it had ever since Juliette left his hotel suite. Regardless, he stayed in his office. And while he hadn't accomplished much, it'd allowed him to avoid his sister, which he'd been doing as much as possible since coming home from Boston.

Either his expression had given him away or Candace had developed mind-reading abilities because she'd known something was wrong when he walked in the kitchen early Sunday afternoon. To her credit, she'd let him share that not only had he put his and Juliette's relationship on hold but his reason for doing so. Once he finished, though, she held nothing back.

She'd been giving him dirty looks or reminding him what

an idiot he was every time she saw him since then. Tonight over dinner wouldn't be any different. Maybe instead of joining Candace and Tiegan, he should sit on Juliette's steps and wait for her to come home.

If he didn't eat for several hours, it wasn't like he'd starve. And if he hung around down there, he'd be guaranteed to see Juliette tonight. Aaron stopped in the driveway and considered the two options.

Mother nature made the decision for him. Lightning streaked across the sky, and the dark clouds that had hovered all day opened up.

"I thought you were still in your office," Candace said as she put a bowl of salad in the middle of the table. "As soon as Mom gets here, we can eat." With the entire campground open for the season, his mom spent a lot more time over in the office and less time here.

Sitting down on a barstool, he grabbed a slice of garlic bread. His sister wasn't Juliette's keeper. They were friends, though, and soon they'd be coworkers, so she might know Juliette's plans for the day and, more importantly, when she'd be back. Then again, if he mentioned Juliette, he risked another lecture where Candace told him what a jerk he was.

Right now, he'd sit through her lecture if it got him the information he wanted.

"I've gone down to the cottage twice today, but Juliette hasn't been there. Did she spend the day at the dance school?" She wanted to get it open as soon as possible. Maybe she'd spent the day setting up her office or something.

"Nope." Candace took a slice of garlic bread from the basket as well.

"Do you know what she was up to today?" Maybe she'd gone furniture shopping. She closed on her new house next week, and she didn't plan to keep the furnishings the home came with.

"Nope," she answered and then proceeded to tear the crust off her bread so she could eat it first—something she'd done for as long as he could remember.

Candace knew more than she was letting on. "Is there anything useful you can tell me?"

"She never came back after you dumped her."

A two-hundred-pound heavyweight boxer punched him the chest.

She is buying a house here. The reminder did nothing to help ease the pain. Most people would be hurt financially if they purchased a home and never moved in. Not Juliette. The same was true about the dance school. She could never return to Avon and not suffer any repercussions.

"I... never mind." There was no point in telling Candace he hadn't dumped Juliette. "Do you know where she went?"

"Maybe."

Strangling his sister wouldn't help, but man, he wanted to right now. "C'mon, Candace. I need to talk to her, and it's not a conversation I want to have over the phone. If you know where she went, please tell me."

"It depends."

"On what?"

"Will the conversation include you telling Juliette you're a first-class moron and getting on your knees and asking her to give you another chance? *Or* are you going to tell her you don't want anything to do with her?"

He'd get on his knees and beg if he had to, but he hoped it didn't come to that. "What do you think?"

Instead of answering, she crossed her arms and studied him. "She went to New York. I'm sure she gave Mom her home address when she reserved the cottage."

Yeah, his mom more than likely had it on the computer, but he wasn't comfortable getting the address that way. He didn't want Candace calling Juliette and asking for it either, because she'd want to know why she wanted it. He'd prefer not to have Juliette tell Candace she didn't want to see him and refuse to give it to her. Although, even if she did, it wouldn't stop him from asking his mom for the address and trying to see her anyway.

"Do you have either Holly or Mrs. Lambert's numbers?"

"Yeah."

"Can you call and get the address from one of them?"

"I'll try Mrs. Lambert after dinner."

Clearly, his sister wanted to punish him tonight. "Candace, come on. Please call one of them now."

"It's already five-thirty, and it's at least a six-hour drive to New York. Even if you left now, by the time you got there, Juliette might be in bed. If you're hoping to get her forgiveness, you shouldn't start by waking her up in the middle of the night."

Candace had a point, but he wouldn't admit it to her. "But if I go tonight, I can check into a hotel and be at Juliette's place first thing in the morning."

She picked up her cell phone on the counter and opened her contact list. "Whatever."

Perhaps he deserved it for being such a jerk on Saturday, but neither Mrs. Lambert nor Holly answered his sister's calls before dinner. Thankfully, Tiegan distracted him enough that he could sit at the table and eat rather than pace around the kitchen. Candace's second call to Mrs. Lambert after they cleared the table and their mom left went unanswered as well, but she got through to Holly. Of course, she made him sit and suffer while they chatted about Juliette's new dance school and the classes Candace would be teaching in the fall. And the next time Candace asked him for a favor, he'd repay her just enough for the torture she put him through since she got him the information.

By the time he had the address and packed an overnight

bag, it was almost seven o'clock. He briefly considered waiting until the morning to leave. If he left now, it'd be well after midnight when he reached the city, but he'd avoid any traffic. More importantly, however, he could be on Juliette's doorstep before breakfast. If he left in the morning, there was no telling how much time the traffic would add to the trip, forcing him to wait even longer to speak with her. In the end, it was a simple decision to make.

"Is this your first time in Manhattan, Mr. Wright?" the gentleman at the desk asked when Aaron arrived at his hotel sometime after one o'clock in the morning.

ON SATURDAY, when she arrived in the city, she'd gone straight to the hospital where she met her two identical twin nieces. Afterward, she'd gone to Scott's condo to relieve her cousin Callie, who'd come by to watch Cooper while Scott and Paige were at the hospital. She'd stayed there until her parents as well as Paige's mom and dad arrived much later that night. She'd had a similar routine for the past three days. She saw today going much the same way.

Carrying her second cup of coffee and a cinnamon-raisin bagel to the table, she joined her sister and brother-in-law. Courtney and Josh had arrived yesterday. Since Paige had stopped working in the middle of April and they didn't expect her to have the babies until next month, Cooper's nanny, who usually watched him while Scott and Paige were gone, had taken a three-week vacation. Since the woman would be away for another week, Courtney and Josh planned to stay and help out until she came back. If Juliette didn't have the closing on Monday and so much to do if she wanted to open the dance school in the fall, she would have remained in the city and helped her brother and sister-in-law too.

"Do you want to relieve Mom and Dad or go to the hospital first?" Courtney asked.

If Scott could split himself in half and be at the hospital and with Cooper at the same time, he would. Since he couldn't, he went to the hospital as early as he could. Usually well before Cooper woke up, and he came home sometime in the late afternoon. Her brother stayed with his son until Cooper went to bed, and then he headed back to the hospital for another brief visit. All that meant that by now, Scott had left, and their parents were watching Cooper.

She adored her nephew and enjoyed spending time with him. Plus, it was impossible to be unhappy around him, a state she'd found herself in often since Saturday. "I'll go over this morning. You'll be with him all next week. Once I go back to Avon, I'm not sure when I'll see him again."

"Sounds good. And before I forget again, has Addie started on the designs for your house?"

Since she could live in the house as it was and she knew Addie had other clients, she'd told Addie to work on the plans when she had the time. Of course, Addie being Addie, she'd started on the plans anyway. "She sent me her ideas for the kitchen. I'll grab my laptop and show you." She took another sip of coffee and stood as her doorbell rang.

"Holly?" Courtney asked.

She shrugged. Holly had stopped by for a little while yesterday.

Juliette opened the door, expecting either Holly or a relative because for anyone else security would have called before allowing them up.

Aaron? Jake's prediction on Saturday replayed in her head, and hope exploded around her heart. It didn't make any sense that he'd drive well over six hours just to tell her he'd decided he didn't want anything else to do with her. Delivering the news over the phone or when she returned to town would be so much easier. Afraid to learn she'd jumped to the wrong conclusion, she asked the second most pressing question she had.

"How did you get in?" *And how did you know where I live?*

"Holly gave my name to security and told them she was expecting me today. She gave Candace your address too."

Had Holly passed along the information before or after her visit? If she'd done it before, she should have told her Aaron planned to come here.

"Can I come in?"

"Yes, of course." She took several steps back so he could enter. "When did you get to Manhattan?" She walked alongside him toward the living room, careful not to let any part of her body touch him, because if even her fingers brushed against his skin, she would be tempted to hug him. And she didn't want to risk being rejected by him.

"Early this morning. I don't know exactly. Maybe around one-thirty or two."

The hope in her chest spread through her body.

"I didn't know you never came back from Boston, and I went down to the cottage twice yesterday to see you. After the second time, I asked Candace if she knew where you were."

"Paige went into labor Saturday afternoon, so I came here." She considered her options of places to sit before picking the sofa.

"How is everyone?" he asked, joining her as she'd hoped he would.

"Paige is fine and will be home today. My nieces are doing well. They were six weeks early, so they're small and will be in the NICU for a little longer. The hospital won't let them come home until they weigh at least four pounds. Except for their low birth weights, they're healthy."

"You were hoping she'd have girls."

Until Saturday, the youngest generation of Sherbrookes and Belmonts had consisted of boys. And as much as she adored her nephew and her cousins' sons, she'd hoped for two nieces. And hopefully, when Courtney gave birth later this year, she'd get a third niece so Scott's twins wouldn't be so outnumbered by their male cousins.

They could talk about her family or any other topic he wanted later. Right now, she wanted him to tell her why he'd driven all the way here in the middle of the night instead of calling her.

"Please don't take this the wrong way, but why are you here? You could have called me or waited until I came back to Avon."

"I didn't want to have this conversation on the phone or wait and see if you came back."

"I told your sister why I was in New York and when I'd be back."

"Yeah, well, she wasn't in a sharing mood," he grumbled before shifting his position, so he was closer to her. "It doesn't matter. Even if I'd known when you'd be back, I wouldn't have been able to wait, and I would've come here. I messed up on Saturday, and I'm sorry. I don't think about what happened to Troy often anymore. When I saw Bryon, it hit me hard." He swallowed and clasped his hands together.

She watched as a mix of emotions played across his face. And as much as she wanted to tell him she understood, she kept quiet rather than interrupt him.

"And sitting there with you surrounded by people that had the same or even more wealth and influence as his family, I assumed they were all the same. That in the same situation, any one of them would get away with what Bryon did. I lumped your family into the group too, and I shouldn't have."

"You're right about some of the people there, but not most."

"It doesn't matter. Who your family associates with doesn't change who you are." He touched her cheek. "Or that I love you."

Jake and Trent were never going to let her forget they were right. Maybe she'd tell them it took Aaron a full week before he knocked on her door so that she could say they weren't 100 percent accurate.

Moving closer, Juliette put her arms over his shoulders and rested her forehead against his. "I'm glad you're here. Whatever you said on Saturday doesn't matter. It's in the past."

She didn't want him changing his mind. At the same time, she remembered Charlie mentioning how she'd found adjusting to the media attention the family often got difficult. She wasn't sure Aaron had considered that at all. If he hadn't, she didn't want it coming up in a month from now and causing him to have second thoughts again.

"Aaron, I love you, *but* I need to ask you something. The media is going to bother you, especially when we go to events like my cousin's wedding or a fundraiser. Some people have a hard time with that. Will you be okay if a picture of us together shows up on the *Star Insider* website or on a magazine cover at Gorham's?"

Instead of answering, he kissed her first. "I think I'll look good on the cover of a magazine."

Well, he had her there. The first time she'd seen him running, hadn't she thought he should be starring in a summer blockbuster with her brother-in-law? "I'm serious, Aaron. I know Charlie had a hard time getting used to the media attention. It most likely won't happen too often since we'll be in Avon, but I guarantee you it will happen."

Aaron slipped his arms around her and kissed her again. "Don't worry. I considered all that."

Good. "I love you." She pressed her lips against his in the briefest of kisses. "And I'd love to stay here with you all day, but I need to watch my nephew so my parents can go to the hospital. Unless you need to get home, I'd like you to come with me."

"The only place I need to be today is with you."

Even if her dad, all her uncles, brother, and male cousins had stood in the room, she wouldn't have been able to stop herself from crushing her lips against his and showing him how much she loved him.

ABOUT THE AUTHOR

USA Today Best Selling author, Christina Tetreault started writing at the age of 10 on her grandmother's manual typewriter and never stopped. Born and raised in Lincoln, Rhode Island, she has lived in four of the six New England states since getting married in 2001. Today, she lives in New Hampshire with her husband, three daughters and two dogs. When she's not driving her daughters around to their various activities or chasing around the dogs, she is working on a story or reading a romance novel. Currently, she has three series out, The Sherbrookes of Newport, Love on The North Shore and Elite Force Security. You can visit her website www.christinatetreault.com or follow her on Facebook to learn more about her characters and to track her progress on current writing projects.

Printed in Great Britain
by Amazon

45948142R00142